what is real

KAREN RIVERS

ORCA BOOK PUBLISHERS

Text copyright © 2011 Karen Rivers

All rights reserved. No part of this publication may be reproduced or transmitted in any form or by any means, electronic or mechanical, including photocopying, recording or by any information storage and retrieval system now known or to be invented, without permission in writing from the publisher.

Library and Archives Canada Cataloguing in Publication

Rivers, Karen, 1970-
What is real / Karen Rivers.

Issued also in electronic format.
ISBN 978-1-55469-356-6

I. Title.
PS8585.I8778W43 2011 JC813'.54 C2010-908046-7

First published in the United States, 2011
Library of Congress Control Number: 2010942087

Summary: When Dex Pratt returns to his small-town life to care for his wheelchair-bound father, he finds his world turned upside down and goes to extreme measures in order to cope.

Orca Book Publishers is dedicated to preserving the environment and has printed this book on paper certified by the Forest Stewardship Council®.

Orca Book Publishers gratefully acknowledges the support for its publishing programs provided by the following agencies: the Government of Canada through the Canada Book Fund and the Canada Council for the Arts, and the Province of British Columbia through the BC Arts Council and the Book Publishing Tax Credit.

Cover design by Teresa Bubela
Typesetting by Jasmine Devonshire
Cover photo by Getty Images
Author photo by Meg VanderLee

ORCA BOOK PUBLISHERS
PO Box 5626, Stn. B
Victoria, BC Canada
V8R 6S4

ORCA BOOK PUBLISHERS
PO Box 468
Custer, WA USA
98240-0468

www.orcabook.com
Printed and bound in Canada.

14 13 12 11 • 4 3 2 1

To you.

chapter 1
now.

This is my real life.

But I keep thinking...

If things were different. In any way. In every way.

If *Before* stretched into *Now*.

Then...

I would still be me.

But it doesn't.

Everything changes.

I am me, but I'm also not myself. I am a guy who is playing himself on TV.

(Except I am not on TV.)

But on the one hand, I'm still trying to get it right: My lines. My *motivation*.

On the other hand, I want to know what is going on here. I have lost something. There is a line that I have crossed, and I can't go back. I didn't cross it. The line crossed me. My mind was crossed.

I am not me.

But what is real?

Are you?

Am I?

Is anyone?

chapter 2
september 26, this year.

EXT.—CORNFIELD—EARLY EVENING, SUNNY

And...

SCENE:

Dex Pratt is on his back in the corn. Eyes half shut. He is holding a spliff. There are shiny scars from old burns on his fingertip because, as it turns out, he isn't very good at this. (Or anything.)

The audience will recognize his character in the first frame. He's that kid.

(Is there more? They won't know that he didn't used to be.)

Close up on the burn scars, the flat shine of his fingertip. The lit ember at the end of the joint. Dex's face. His red-veined, pink-high eyes. The stain of the smoke.

Pan the field. Pan the blue-fading-to-gray sky, messy with clouds. Back to Dex on his back, sweating through his shirt. His T-shirt is ripped: Che's face gapes open from ear to chin. His shorts are not exactly clean. Below the frayed hem, his left knee bulges purple-gray, yellow-green, a bruised fruit, throbbing with pain.

Focus on the joint, burning, the ash as he raises it slowly to his lips, the long slow pull of it. And then the lips, sealed shut, holding it all in.

(Hold it all in, that's what he does, isn't it?)

Because.

Now there is the wind blowing through the corn, making sounds like ghosts or someone so sad that his pain becomes a low sound.

Add a layer of music. No words, just some flutes dismally whistling spit through silver tubes. No, violins. The whine of the strings.

Show how Dex is hearing the ghosts in the corn, and the pot is high and...no, wait, that's the corn. His eyes are open. No, closed. The corn is high in the maze. The maize maze. The corn maze that frames him, walls holding him in, walls trapping him here.

In this town.

In this life, which is not his.

But it is.

Our Joe's maze is built out of lies and funds more lies. There is no money in corn or there is. The money is in the maze or maybe Our Joe just likes kids getting lost in there, crying. That is close to a truth that Dex doesn't want to know. Look away, look away. Show a bull's-eye. Show Dex, looking away. Don't let your eyes settle on what you don't want to know, because there is a point at which it is too much, and sometimes a maze is just a way of getting high-school kids to part with ten bucks to scare the shit out of themselves.

But…

And…

Then.

There is something about Our Joe that Tanis said. There is something. Show Dex trying to think of what it is, without looking at the obvious thing that he knows but can't deal with.

Show how Dex can't deal.

What does that look like? Crying?

No.

It doesn't show.

Asshole.

Show a shadow in the corn. The shadow of a child, running.

Show Dex in the corn, standing. No, sitting. No, lying down.

Show Dex not helping.

But then, like a lot of Dex's thoughts, it slips away, and what Tanis said is a bird. Show the bird flying through the maze, toward the center. Away from Dex. Show the bird in the center of the maze turning into a child with a crooked face, crying.

Show Dex shaking his head. Blank. He was thinking something. What was it? It was something about Our Joe.

Bile rises in Dex's throat. Show Dex spitting on the ground. In the bubbles of the spit, show the shape of the bird and the thing he is forgetting, which is important, but what is it?

Show Dex inhaling and inhaling and inhaling and never ever, ever exhaling and the ember burning orange-red. Show how that is suffocating him, like his mom used to when she slept with him, wrapped around him so tightly he couldn't breathe. Show him struggling for air.

FLASHBACK TO:

INT.—CHILD'S ROOM

Show Young Dex, sleeping. Pan his room, all the stuff of a regular boy who laughs so hard he pees, sometimes, and even that is funny. Show plastic toys, Star Wars *posters, books, stuffed animals. Show his mom's lips in his hair. Show her whispering. Show him smiling in his sleep.*

Show happy. Can you show "happy"?

How?

CUT BACK TO PRESENT:

And then to the now, Dex's face a blank place where smiles don't quite fit.

Then...

All of a sudden!

The scene is interrupted.

DEX

Huh?

It's light.

Really light.

Eyes open now.

DEX

What the fuck?

He either says that out loud or he doesn't. Inhales tight. Holds it. Then the gallons of smoke escape from his lips like something liquid.

(He is losing control of this. But that seems to happen a lot lately. He starts it, and it goes from there.)

In the corn, the light is so intense to no longer even be light but something more. Dex can't open his eyes. He can, he does, and then slams them closed again. He can't see. He is blind and he isn't. The light is. It just IS.

So obviously he is dead.

Dex is dead.

DEX

I am not fucking dead.

VOICE-OVER

Everything is an illusion.

(But who is doing the goddamn voice-over? Dex's movies don't have voice-overs. Or at least he hasn't done any with voice-overs yet.)

Dex isn't dead. But maybe this isn't his movie, after all.

Dex is in the cornfield on his back, getting high. Except that he isn't. And the light is going right through him, and he's lifted. He's up in it, on it, under it, within it, a vacuum of it, and he's spinning. And there is something in his mouth that tastes like pennies and dog hair. And he can't breathe the air because it is thick like snot, and he can't breathe, he can't breathe, he can't breathe.

He's sick.

Gagging on the air. Dry heaving himself inside out. A somersault, then four more. His torso is twisting in a way that is not possible, his whole body being wrung out.

And Dex is slammed down hard on concrete ground—where?

Somewhere else.

He's bleeding. He must be, but he can't tell; red isn't visible here. Now. What happened to red? His bones broken, or not, his tongue somewhere misplaced, the place pitch-white, not black. Nothing is black. He yearns for black in a way he's never yearned for anything before.

The ground is wet and sticky.

There are people crying. Children. A hiccupping sob that isn't him. It isn't the corn; it isn't the sad wail of the corn ghosts. Or it is? He can't see. He can. Shadows in the mist. And what is this?

Aliens.

He's crazy. This can't be real. But then there is the ground and the pain and the wetness and a ringing in his head and something...

Someone. That he isn't making up.

Imaginary things don't hurt like this, a pain that sings through him and makes him think, absurdly, of how mermaids lured sailors into the deep.

The seductive big eyes of...

The thing in front of him is...

All eyes. (He saw this once in a movie, a real one. The oil-pool sliding surface of eyes so big you can fall into them. And then he thinks of the tar pits and the dinosaurs forever frozen in the black, sinking ground. And he thinks maybe he understands something, suddenly, about prehistory that he's never understood before. But that could be the weed, is the weed, must be the...)

His head hurts; his brain is too big or too small or exploding or imploding. The aliens are two plate-sized eyes and nothing more...colors sliding around too fast, a gale storm on an oil puddle in a parking lot. He's crazy. That's it, he's lost it.

The creature is waist-high, its eyes the size of Dex's own head. Its head the size of a pillow.

Dex doesn't even like sci-fi.

He doesn't believe in this.

He was only imagining.

Is only imagining.

DEX

I am making this up.

He feels around for the ground. For the corn.

Then a hand is on his left knee. A hand-like shape. A human hand. A non-human hand. It's white but it isn't. It's whiter than all that white light and somehow less solid—liquid, cold. Something metallic smooth, pressing hard inside his knee, inside his purple, blue-black knee, sinking into his skin like a faith healer tearing a chicken heart from a believer.

The blood is red.

Dex throws up. (Suddenly. For real.) Show Dex throwing up. Everything he's ever eaten. A volcano powerful enough to make islands in the earth. Molten.

He is on fire.

He is fire.

The burn will kill him. It has to kill him.

So he's dead then.

He falls.

Into the soft, soft dirt. He becomes a valley, which rises up and becomes a crevasse, which softens to a dent and thrusts him upward. His body is an outline.

Dex Pratt is on his back in the cornfield. The stars are out, flattened cornstalks all around.

He either is or is not dead.

DEX

Not.

He either imagined this or didn't.

He stands up and he runs. The running feels like flying. Or skating. It is so smooth. Too smooth. Oiled-metal smooth, ball-bearings smooth, ice smooth, dream smooth.

He runs back to the ramshackle half-house where he lives with his dad, perched there on the back of Our Joe's cornfield like an afterthought, but older than the corn, so really a beforethought.

FLASHBACK TO:

EXT.—THE OLD HOUSE—WINTER

DAD

Original means old. Old is the new New.

(laughing)

Isn't that what your mother would say?

DEX

Dad, it's a shithole. We can't live here. There's snow in the living room.

DAD

(shaking hands with Our Joe)

Yes, we can. And now we do.

OUR JOE

Welcome home, kid.

DEX

Great. This is just perfect.

CUT BACK TO PRESENT:

Dex runs from the frame. The herky-jerky camera that doesn't exist tries to keep up.

His legs are new. His lungs are new. He's alive.

Or at least not dead.

Is it the same thing?

There is lightning somewhere, but there isn't. It's in him. It is him.

He falls, runs, stumbles, finds himself on the porch, sweating.

DAD

That you?

DEX

Me. Who else would it be?

DAD

Never know, kid. You never know.

Pan down Dex's body, soaked with sweat. Shaking. Focus tight on his knee. His left knee. Show how it is unmarked.

And also, how it doesn't hurt.

Also how the purple, swollen bruising is gone and the skin glows white.

Seriously.

What the FUCK?

There is no such thing as ALIENS.

And all that is Mrs. D's fault. And T-dot's. And Tanis's. And Olivia's.

Behind him, the corn is flattened.

In front of him, his dad is a shadow through the screen door.

And...

CUT.

It was real.

Or was it?

chapter 3
september 1, this year.

My life used to be a glass pitcher of white, pure, clean, delicious milk just bubbling over with goddamn *wholesomeness*. My entire life. My whole family was shiny and perfect, snipped right out of the stereotype catalogue: Mom, Dad, me, Chelsea, and our loyal dog, Glob. We had a fish in a bowl on the granite kitchen counter and a ride-on lawnmower and shiny new bikes for our birthdays and five food groups a day and family fucking *game* night on Wednesdays. We had a stainless-steel barbecue the size of a small car and an above-ground pool. Friends slept over and we had our own tents in the backyard during the endless summer months–an interminable paradise of boredom and adventure and safe predictability.

I'm seventeen now, and that's all gone. Seventeen doesn't sound old. But it is. Trust me.

What can I tell you?

A lot happened. Most of it was inevitable. I just didn't see it coming.

I learned to read when I was three years old. Maybe every book is a lifetime. Maybe it is the fault of the books and not the fault of everything else. That I'm so old. That I got so fucking old.

But I don't believe that. Do you?

There's a home movie of me riding down the street on my BMX bike, a book taped to the handlebars. I'm grinning at the camera, two teeth missing, freckled nose, messy hair sticking out from under my orange flame-painted helmet. I look like a goddamn commercial for back-to-school clothes or chewable vitamins. I ride right into the person holding the camera and the camera gets dropped and you hear my dad's voice saying, "Dex!" and then the laughter is all you hear and you see my sneaker and some gravel and that's it.

It's over.

When people asked, "What are you going to be when you grow up?"

"A writer-director," I answered. And they'd be surprised because, if you didn't know me, you'd take me for a kid who would say "fireman" or "hockey player."

But I had a plan. A fucking great *plan*.

My plan was to be the guy they talked about in the *New York Times* and argued about on the Internet. But then they'd love me anyway because my stories would be so amazing that they wouldn't be able to help themselves. I'd write movies and books and everything everything everything because that's how I felt when I was a kid. Like everything was waiting to be created.

By me.

My great master plan was to be: Funny. Smart. Happy. Popular.

That's what I wanted to be when I grew up.

Was that too much to ask?

I wanted to grow up to be the guy who got the girl. The Girl. Even now, thinking about it, I don't know if the whole plan was to get to the part with the girl or if the girl was just a part of the plan. A detail.

She was one specific imaginary girl. I sound like an asshole, but I'll say it anyway. Why not? I have nothing to lose. I have nothing to hide.

The girl was the *prize*. My prize. That I'd earn by being a big-shot celebrity. That's the truth.

I made up every part of her: fine blond hair that swooped to her waist, wavy like she was just surfing, even though there's no surf around here. Big eyes, glasses like mine, quirky. Skin like porcelain. A brain like a whip. Always a book in her hand, her hands with pale pink nails. Four freckles on her left cheek. Vegetarian. Great taste in music. Plays a guitar and has a good singing voice.

The whole package. The kind of girl who would have a place in New York but would also hike the Himalayas. The kind of girl who would never live in this town, no way. The kind of girl who knew how to leave and not look back. An artsy girl. A hippie chick. Someone *other*. Someone unreal. A model. An actress. Someone with that glow. Better than. Hotter. Smarter. Someone who understood that no matter where you were, you were alone and you were you. And someone who was okay with that.

Someone who the guy with the award, the books, the movie camera—that guy—would *deserve*.

She was specific. A specific person who didn't exist. The fantasy changed a lot—the type of movies I'd make, for example—but the girl was always the same. And you know, the older I got, the more The Girl became The Plan and The Plan itself was about The Girl.

I was totally in love with the girl. Crazy, fucked up, right? Maybe that's when it started to slip away.

It.

Me.

Maybe that's when *I* started slipping away.

It's not my fault. All I did was believe. You're supposed to believe, right? What the adults say. So I did. I believed all the lies about how "You can be whatever you want to be, son. Dream it and you can become it." Now I want to go back in time and punch myself in the jaw. I want to break my bones. I want to smash myself until I understand.

It's all *bullshit*. Carefully crafted bullshit, but still bullshit. Like Santa and the Easter bunny and love.

Maybe I knew it was bullshit, and I just didn't care. I was in love with myself. My future self. I was in love with that imaginary girl.

With The Girl on my arm, I'd win prizes. My speeches would be short and funny. My tux would be *cerulean*. I'd wear it with a T-shirt underneath. (I'd no sooner wear a collared shirt than I'd wear a ball gown.) I would have three days' stubble. I would refuse to comb my hair. In this footage of me, I'm not the real me, but a trumped-up movie-star version of me that only really resembles *me* at one angle in a particularly flattering photo.

The only part of my great dream that came true was the glasses, the "I'm a writer; I'm famous" glasses. I wear them, even though the rest of it is as likely to happen as the polar ice caps refreezing. The glasses are so pretentious; they make me hate myself just *that* much more.

I used to be so stupid. How can anyone that stupid actually survive?

They can't.

Bam.

I'm dead.

So yeah, when I look back on *before*, I see myself skipping through a meadow singing *tra-la-la* so loudly that I missed all the obvious things about life, such as, "It never turns out the way you expect, young asshole."

But you can see how I got it wrong, right?

I mean, I was so cute. And smart. And back then, my dad grew *tomatoes* in the basement.

Dad loved those tomatoes, red and green and yellow, some of them as big as a baby's head. We ate them constantly, raw and covered with salt. Cooked in sauces. Sliced in sandwiches. Fried. Mom canned them—we had rows and rows of glass jars in the basement, full of red flesh. It would probably make a better story if I hated tomatoes or was allergic to them or worse. But I loved them. We all did. Dad especially. I don't know how a person gets into *tomatoes*, but he sure was. He took care of them better than he took care of us, and he was okay at that too. He just loved the tomatoes more.

And my mom. He loved my mom. The joke was on him, though, because it turned out she loved some other guy she met on the Internet who claimed to love sailing and travel and *her*. A politician with striped ties and a tuft of hair sticking out the back of the collar of his shirt. I guess that canning tomatoes and living with us weren't her thing after all, although she faked it pretty well all that time.

Some people are better actors than others.

Maybe I get that from her.

Maybe.

So she left Dad and became someone else, someone unrecognizable. She morphed as easily as a caterpillar. But we were the cocoon that had to be torn open so she could become some kind of creepy, unrecognizable butterfly, flying away.

You don't really heal from that.

I look at Mom now and I can hardly remember her living in this town. Going to her job at the bank every day, driving past the farmers' fields that she was going to repossess. It's a different place now. All the farms have signs at the ends of the driveways. Corporate signs. *Proudly Growing Corn for______! Proud Supplier to______.*

Yeah, I bet they're proud. But signs that say, *Forced to Sell Soul to the Corporate Devil* and *Proud to Genetically Modify Corn for Profit* tend to make people uncomfortable.

I can conjure up certain memories of Mom being here: the *clip-clop* of her high heels on the polished wood floors. The screech of her brakes when she stopped in the driveway because she was always in such a hurry that she sometimes forgot to slow down in time and she'd hit the garage door with her front bumper.

But I try to picture her and I can't. Her face keeps getting away from me, and even when I watch the old videos,

I can't quite see her clearly. It's like she's got that blurred-out spot over her face the whole time. Somehow she's never in focus. I try and try and try to really see her, but as soon as the screen flickers off, she's gone again, like a slippery dream you can't keep in your mind after you've woken up. I don't think she was ever really here. That's the thing. This was the detour in her life plan. This wasn't *it*.

Here's a moral: Plans are a waste of time.

I watch those stupid movies over and over again, until one day I just stop.

My dad changed too, but that'll happen after you try to kill yourself and fail. That, by the way, is a real slap in the face to your kid. Maybe think about that if you're ever perched naked on the top of a grain elevator, contemplating all the different ways to get down.

Dad stopped thinking about me sometime around the day I moved to Vancouver and started going to St. Joe's Academy. Mom wasn't the only caterpillar. I was a hick kid from a hick town, but I polished up okay and flew just fine. Maybe I was a moth though. I preferred the night to the day. I flew into the flames all the time.

I did all right there. He said I was different, and I was, but I wasn't bad-different yet. Just different. No, scratch that.

You are always *you*, right? No matter where the fuck you live. But I was happy. It felt easy to be that version of me. Worse, it felt better. Shinier. Brighter. I got mixed up. I thought rich meant "more important."

Does money change you?

Stupid question. But hey, it turned out that I loved sailing and travel too. Is that so shocking?

Dad said he could see the city on my face when I came home. And I don't know what the fuck he was talking about, but I will say that my skin was better (Accutane) and I had way nicer clothes and a haircut that wasn't done by the barber on Main Street. I was fit as hell, my body as hard as steel. That's true too. But I don't think that's what he meant.

He said I was my mother's son. That was supposed to be an insult, right?

I didn't know for sure. He loved my mom. So maybe it wasn't.

Thinking about it tears a hole in me wide enough that I can see through me. That's how it feels.

Love.

What a joke.

Speaking of jokes, Dad used to be a lawyer. A *lawyer*. It's all he ever wanted to be, and that's what he was. Dad had that kind of life. He'd pick something (the house, Mom, a career, kids) and then he'd get it. He just kept plodding forward and getting what he wanted, and even if he wasn't happy, he sure looked it.

Now he cries during sitcoms and pees into a bag that's taped to his chair. And he grows *marijuana*. If our house burns down, everyone within a mile will be high for a week and the insurance won't even begin to cover the cost of all the burnt cash.

And you thought the tomatoes were impressive.

I say *he* grows marijuana because that's what he believes. The truth is that *I* grow marijuana. Because only one of us can make it down the cellar stairs, and it isn't the guy in the shiny new wheelchair.

So now look at my life:

The milk in that glass jug is curdled. It's yellow and spongy and you'd as soon gag as look at it. And don't even think about taking a sniff. The thing with milk is that you can't uncurdle it. It can't ever go back to what it was.

I'm a different person. I'm not the person I was meant to grow up to be when we lived in a four-bedroom colonial in a subdivision outside of town. I'm not the laughing kid who would never shut up and thought he'd be a star. I'm not the smart, funny, athletic, popular, all-star, wake-up-smiling kid.

I'm not even the in-between guy—the rich, artsy, pretentious, prep-school one who lived in Vancouver with his mom and her new husband, with his little sister and his stepbrother, in a house made of glass that hung over the edge of a cliff like it was mocking nature. The one who visited his dad for a week in the summer and two days over Christmas break in the farm town where he grew up and thought, Man, this place is sad. I'll never move back.

Never say never.

Now I'm the teenaged, pissed-off, raging stoner who fails hard and who lives with his broken dad in a broken house on the back acre of Our Joe's corn farm and sleeps on a mattress stuffed with money that can't ever go into the bank.

Actual money. Mostly twenty-dollar bills.

Money smells. Did you know that? It stinks of must and ink and other people's hands and a life you don't want to have.

I could take the money and go, but where would I go? I might sound like a jerk but I'm not the kind of jerk who would leave his broken dad behind. Not yet anyway.

I used to use words like *cerulean* because I liked how it felt in my mouth. Now I just say *blue*.

Why bother saying things you have to explain?

That's who I am now. Someone who doesn't explain.

And I'm sure as hell not the guy who grows up, follows The Plan and gets The Girl. That guy took a different turn in the maze and got out a long time ago. Whereas I'm still in here, looking for something I never wanted to find.

chapter 4
september 5, this year.

I am slumped on my bed, staring out the window at the sprawl of the cornfield, and I don't know who I am here or what to do with my hands, but here I am.

I am Dex Pratt. I am seventeen years old. I am living at home with my dad. I have a girlfriend. I have friends. Summer is winding down and school is about to begin. I don't have to know more than this, but I want to know more than this. I feel like I'm watching a movie and everyone else knows something about the plot, the key to it, and I don't know it. Or I was in the bathroom when the secret was revealed and now I'm just watching.

Except it's more like the movie is watching me.

I am the movie.

It's like that.

My dad and I run out of things to say to each other and the air is full of my lies and his depression. And I go down to the basement and I take more pot, and more and more and more pot, and I buy rolling papers in bulk on the Internet. And I go into the corn. I go lie in the corn. And I've lost track of what day it is, but what does it matter? The movies come whether I want them to or not. And I lie on my back in the cornfield and right below me are the worms and grubs and maggots, seething through the dirt. And above me is the blinding white ball of the sun and the shadows that are being thrown down on me by the endless stalks of corn. And down there, I *am* the grub. I am the dirt. I am the ground. And I don't have to be Dex Pratt, age seventeen, troubled kid. I can just sink until there are no spaces between my molecules anymore and there is no difference between me and the dirt. The grubs and the worms are *me*.

It's my safe place. That's how shrinks talk, you know. They want you to find your "safe place."

Mine is on the ground. In the ground, maybe. Safe, safe. Held up. Held down.

So that is where I go, screen door banging behind me. Phone buzzing in my pocket. Dad yelling, "When are you coming home?"

Me leaving.

EXT.—CORNFIELD—EARLY AFTERNOON, SUNNY WITH LOOSE CLOUDS

Dex's mental film is shaky today, all Blair Witch Project *heavy breathing and a wobbling lens. A Tilt-A-Whirl effect complete with nausea and sweating. People hate that. So they say, but they always watch it.*

Dex breathes.

His heart is crooked. His head is crooked. This shit is making him feel crooked. He keeps forgetting to ask Gary what is different about this weed. Gary has done something. Something has changed.

Is it different or just more?

More and more. And, fuck it, MORE.

Show how Dex is smoking more and more. Splice together a hundred scenes, fast, of Dex with a jay in his hand, in his mouth, in his hand, rolling and smoking, and smoking and rolling, and how fast his fingers go. Speed up the film. Speed it up and speed it up until it blurs and melts.

Not that film really melts anymore. Not like that.

Add the lie of melting.

Because, truth is, there is never enough for Dex to fully blot it all out, you understand? Everyone says that pot blurs the edges, but it doesn't. Not for Dex. The edges of his life are as sharp as knife blades cutting through the air and leaving behind wounded oxygen molecules, bleeding red into the blue.

Focus.

Dex is on his back.

In the cornfield.

And no one knows where he is.

And no one cares.

Somehow show that no one cares. A shot of Dad (INT.—KITCHEN TABLE) hunched over the kitchen table, building another house; show his hands moving the tiny refrigerator closer to the tiny stove, the squint of his eyes, the way he is holding his breath until the angle is just right. Then the dilated pupils, a slow shot of the wheelchair and the bottles of pills that are never out of his reach. Then his wasted legs. The golden bag of piss. The soles of the new white shoes, brand-new shoes that have never touched the ground.

Then cut away. Dizzyingly. Like something being dropped.

FLASHBACK TO:

EXT.—GRAIN ELEVATOR

Show Dad standing at the top of the grain elevator, the blue sky arcing above him without any clouds. (Were there clouds?) Show the heat, shimmering like translucent wings, the nearly transparent melting of everything real into the scribbled blur of sky.

It was too much sky, maybe that was it.

He is naked except for his shoes. Show that.

Show Mom laughing with SD in Vancouver, maybe in front of a landmark to make it recognizable. Show them holding hands. She's wearing sunglasses. Her hair is perfectly cut, razor sharp, swinging. Show SD's teeth and how they look like the teeth of a dog, long and yellow, blackened rims. Show Mom's toothpaste-white, perfect (new) teeth. And her high-heeled shoes. A color: expensive dusty blue. Show Dad's mouth, unsmiling. No teeth showing. Show his shoes too. Worn leather loafers. Brown. No socks.

Where are his clothes?

Mom laughing and laughing and laughing. Nothing in the world is that funny, lady. Dex needs to tell her: You're overplaying your part, ma'am.

The woman playing the part of Mom does not take direction.

Fire her.

Back to Dad. How did he get up there? He's standing on the top of a grain elevator, poised like he's about to tag it with spray paint but he doesn't have a can. His hands are empty. Clenched. Not clenched. One of each.

Definitely there should be wind ruffling his hair. Show how all that air felt on his skin. How can you show that? You can't. Show the air and his skin, the small hairs on his arms rising and falling. Show how the air is like water, a current. His facial expression is...Blank? A small smile playing at his lips? (How did he feel? In that moment?) Is he looking up or down? Is he crying? Is he pissed off? Does he shake his fist at the endless dome of the sky, framing his sad, lonely life in oversaturated blue?

Does he bother?

No, he's just there.

Show the SOLD sign on the old house. The U-Haul truck with all his belongings parked at the base of the grain elevator.

Show him climbing the ladder.

Show the climb.

Then, at the top.

He is probably, maybe, (actually, not) crying and crying and crying, and everything in the world is that sad. (He should be crying but he isn't.)

Cut back and forth between Mom's face and Dad's, closer and closer. Zoom right in to their eyes like the camera is a goddamn mosquito, buzzing closer and closer. Happy, sad, happy, sad, happy, sad, happy, sad, happy, until the audience is sick from it. A frenetic, background song that's all percussion and ear-splitting cymbals and discordant bangs on some kind of church organ.

Then stop suddenly.

Show Dad jumping. Or falling. No, STEPPING. (An important distinction. Did he reach down for the ground or reach up for the sky? Which way was he looking? Were his eyes open or closed? Did he lie back into the fall or swan-dive for the ground?)

Don't overthink it, Dex, for Pete's sake. It's enough.

So.

He dives. Holding his breath. It is water. The thing with corn is that it looks that way, from a distance. Like an ocean.

No soundtrack.

Add the sound of Glob, barking. Waiting for Dad to land. Bark, bark. The thud of the impact. The dog sniffing him, then running. Like Lassie. Getting help.

Then pan into the distance, the wind moving the corn and maybe some birds chirping.

Then show the wheelchair again, the highly polished silver shine of it. Then show the city where Mom lives. The highly polished silver shine of that. (It should be raining in the city. Vancouver shines in the rain. At night. Slick black roads.) Show the slick black leather of the wheelchair's seat.

And...

CUT.

chapter 5
september 6, this year.

It is the first day of school, twelfth grade. It's meant to be exciting, but it feels like the end of everything. Something has to come next, after, and I have nothing.

No plans.

No goals.

No fucking dreams.

Just this. This rainy, dreary, depressing day. And I have to get myself to the illustrious Main Street School in the center of town within the next fourteen minutes or else. Everything is far here, even though the town is small. Main Street School is miles away. The farms make the whole place spread out like butter on toast, and our place—Our Joe's place—drips right off near the edge. I'm going to have to pedal hard to make it, but I'm fast and fit so I probably can.

Maybe.

If I cared.

The thing is that it's raining and the "or else" doesn't mean anything more than nothing. Even though school is better than home, I can't make myself go.

What is the *point*?

For a split second, I am my dad on the grain elevator, and suddenly the sky is the ground and I've fallen. But I'm not going to kill myself, because that would be easy and obvious. And besides, I don't want to die. I just want to be someone else.

I *can* be someone else.

I *am* someone else.

I look in the mirror and try to see myself. The mirror is dirty. I *look* fine. I am not sick. I do not need to be at home. Gary is already here, walking heavily around the living room, boots on. He never takes them off, leaves mud everywhere. It pisses me off, the soles of his boots leaving diamonds of shit all over the wood floors.

But he's here.

So, *fine*.

Kids who are fine go to school. They do normal shit. They are normal and they are *fine*. But I do not believe that I am fine. I know I am not. This is not right.

I am not right.

I look like I always look—hair, eyes, cheeks, nose, lips, teeth, idiotic glasses that remind me of who I am not and never will be.

I practice smiling like a normal person. Like someone who has something to smile about. I show all my teeth, which are straight and even and white, and I try to make my eyes move accordingly.

Fail.

If I had fangs, I'd be a vampire, trying to look human and not succeeding, fooling no one, dead by the end of the first scene.

I am an asshole in a bright blue T-shirt advertising a band that I've never heard play. My eyes are red and flat and have too many veins and too-small pupils. The dust on the mirror is thick and gray. I use my finger to smear a smiley face into it and successfully fight the urge to punch it with my fist just to feel something.

I have to simmer down. I can't always be on a low boil. But I am.

Something huge is *missing* but it's not obvious what it is, unless it's just whatever switch is needed to change from hot-headed to calm and cool.

I kick the dresser, probably breaking my toe. The mirror shakes but doesn't break.

I touch my hair, my lips, my skin. I have a zit on my cheek that hurts, just below the skin, waiting to be ugly. I need to shave. When I rub my stubble, I feel old. How did I get so old?

I touch my eyebrows. My forehead. The skin of my eyelids. I clean my glasses. I stare hard at the stretched hole in my ear and take out the stretcher and replace it with an ammonite plug, which both hurts and doesn't. It's disgusting and it's not. I like the pulling feeling of my flesh as the cold stone slides in.

I used to think that ammonites were dinosaur snails. But when I was a kid, I would never have had a hole stretched so wide in my earlobe that I could jab one in there for decoration.

When I was a kid...

I *am* a fucking kid. Aren't I?

Old people start to lose things, right? Their memory. Brain cells. Spinal fluid.

I am losing things, but not those particular things. I'm shedding pieces of me like someone with some kind of invisible leprosy.

One of the first things I lost was "funny." Feral took that with him on March 16 last year when he stuck that needle into his arm and then looked up at me, eyes sleepy, and smiled and said, "Ahhh." Like he had never been so *relieved* in his life. And just like that, I lost him forever.

My brother.

Me.

Gone.

I will never be funny again.

My dad took a bunch of me when he decided to jump. When he thought about it. When he didn't say goodbye.

When he drove himself to the elevator. When he climbed to the top.

I think he was doing it *to* me. He was probably hoping for "sad" or "sorry," but I stopped caring about anything on March 16, so it was his bad luck that by June 30, I no longer gave enough of a shit to be sad.

I am losing my ability to tell what is real from what I've made up. That's the scariest one. Cue the crazy-guy music. I haven't told anyone. Who would I tell? Dad?

As if.

I should tell Tanis. I could tell Tanis. I won't tell Tanis. She wouldn't get it. Or, worse, she would. I don't want her to. Tanis is smarter than me. She is smarter than everyone. She is smart enough to not be my girlfriend. And I need her so bad that I can't tell her the truth or anything. I can just hold on tight to her body and tell her all the things she wants to hear just to make her stay right there, holding me up without knowing she's holding me up. And I swear to god I would die without her and I don't even love her or really even know her. And I don't want to, it's like that.

Enough, I say to myself. Stop. It's *enough*.

I'm late. I need to hurry. My heart is racing like it's already rushing. But I sit down on the edge of my bed. My sheets stink because I never bother to wash them. My room is dark because opening the curtains is mostly too much trouble and I don't want to see the goddamn corn.

So now it's like the room itself has accumulated extra darkness, storing it in the corners and under the bed.

There are a bunch of dishes on the floor. There is something that looks a lot like mouse shit in the shadows.

I open my laptop because I can't help it. There are stickers all over it advertising brands of skis. I can't remember why I stuck them there or which brand I liked best or really what it felt like to ski. Most of the stickers are half worn off, ripped. Wrecked. Like me.

I can't stop myself from doing this, from opening it, even though there is so much here I should delete. I shouldn't have a laptop anymore. I don't use it for anything except this. I don't check my mail or Facebook or any other fucking thing. I don't look at YouTube or play games or update my goddamn status. Instead, I open my video library, but I never watch the films. Not anymore. It's enough to see the dates. The tiny squares. The things I could watch if I wanted to.

Which I don't.

I have lots of footage. Mostly of me and Feral, being us. The lame band we cobbled together that "everyone" said would probably make it big. How we sort of believed it. You can see it when we're playing, our faces taking it a little too seriously, considering it sounded like shit.

The laughing, the amount of *laughing*, you'd think that life was just the most hilarious thing. You'd think that it was a TV show and everyone was good-looking and happy. And eventually you'd change the channel because all that happiness could get boring and you might not realize, wait, there is more going on here. Things are about to get ugly.

Look, my so-called talk show:

Me: Tell me what you're going to do with your life, young man.

Feral: I'm going to…STAR IN IT. (Canned laughter and applause; Feral runs around the stage doing a victory lap.)

Me: And what will that get you?

Feral: Laid! (More canned laughter.)

The real-life footage:

School neckties flapping in the wind in the Saab convertible Feral got for his sixteenth. My girlfriend, Glass, her hair pale purple and silky, looking like one of the commercials she'd starred in, spitting the wind-whipped hair out of her mouth, fake lips sticky with fruit-smelling gloss. Laughing eyes.

Then we're at the mountain, in the lodge. The white glare of the snow outside. All that money made us think we were adults. All that money made people treat us like adults. Fucking idiots. What they let us get away with.

We were sixteen. It was spring. The last snow before the ski season ended. The mountain was white but the sky was blue.

I am learning to hate blue sky.

The fire was orange. We all had red, sunburned cheeks. The music was loud and livid. People were dancing and making out. There was the flash of someone's tits. There was a needle in Feral's arm.

It was my birthday. March 16.

The song that was playing. What was it?

There was the way I kept filming. What kind of asshole keeps filming?

"*You*," I say to myself, sitting on the edge of my disgusting bed, late for school. The sheets are wet from my sweat. "You are the asshole," I say.

The way he died.

What do you do with video footage of your favorite person, your fucking brother, doing *that*?

So yeah.

I hold up a pretend camera on my shoulder. I point it at the mirror.

"Take a good look at yourself, Dex Pratt," I say out loud. "What you're missing might be your soul."

That sounds funny and also not. Funny enough that you laugh. But it comes out like a kid's hiccuping sob.

You are silent. You stare at yourself.

You know the truth:

You left yourself in Vancouver in the garbage can in the airport, where you chucked the bag containing your camera—the fucking amazing camera that you loved—on your way back to Nowhere, BC, to look after your dad, fresh out of rehab and ready to live on his own. "His own" meaning "with you." Like doing that kind of penance was going to save you.

Almost ten months ago, exactly.

Are you saved yet?

Taking care of Dad is a whole world outside of what you thought you'd ever do, ever be asked to do. Yes, you *offered*, but you thought someone would stop you. Didn't you?

You can't even take care of yourself.

The airport smelled like a hospital.

You pretend not to be angry but you can't help it. How can you help it? Or maybe you are pretending *to* be angry. It's hard to tell anymore.

Think of something funny, quick.

But nothing is funny.

"Stop it," I say to myself, dropping my pretend camera. "Shut up. Shut your fucking brain up. You *will* go to school. You *will* play basketball. You *will* be normal."

But what else?

You *will* run a grow-op in the basement of your rented house.

Your dad *will* sell drugs through an "organization."

You *will* look in the mirror every fucking morning and try to remember who you are.

Now go, get on your bike and go to school. You *command* yourself to go. "Get on your bike and go to school. NOW."

I go.

My bike is light. It weighs nothing. It skims through the puddles, and the spray of water and shit goes up my back. Mud crusts over the concert dates on my shirt. I ride faster and faster, the bike gripping and then slipping in the mud, and I want to fall but I don't. I take the shortcut through Maxim's land, a dirt tractor road ripped deeply with tread marks, and my bike looks like it's been dipped in chocolate. The mud sprays thick and far, and the ruts are so deep they hammer me up and down, like riding down stairs. I go faster and faster until it feels like I'm flying.

I'm cold and soaked with sweat, but by the time I get to school, I feel almost like myself again. Or so I say to myself.

I am the director.

I am the writer.

I am the actor.

It's funny though—the one thing I never wanted to do was act.

chapter 6
september 6, still.

I walk into the school twenty-two minutes late, out of breath, heart pounding, stinking. The halls are empty, which is the way I like it. For some reason, crowds make me nervous. They make me think of maggots. Fat white worms swarming over something dead. I never used to think like this and now I can't stop.

Things like the maggots. Why am I thinking about maggots?

I don't even hate maggots. I like to know they are there, under the dirt.

Waiting.

Oh, fuck you, Dex.

I think about maggots, and then I wish there was a crowd. At least Tanis. Or T-dot. T-dot was my best friend when we were kids. I went to Vancouver. He stayed here.

I changed.

He stayed the same.

The thing is that he wouldn't understand about the maggots.

Tanis might. But Tanis would have been on time for class. Tanis is a girl who is on time for things.

The emptiness in the hallway is freaking me out. My breath is loud and scratchy, and my mouth is as dry as sandpaper. I stop at the fountain and drink gum-flavored water until I'm sputtering. I come up coughing.

I go to the office to grab my schedule from the wooden tray on the front desk labeled *SCHEDULES*. Someone's turned the heat up too high in here and my glasses steam up and I'm already overheated and sweat runs into my eyes. I practice breathing normally. The air is muddy and too thick. I am probably gasping, so it's lucky there is no one there. I concentrate on the paper.

The paper is pale pink with my name at the top, handwritten. *Dex Pratt!* Exclamation point! The whole schedule is peppered with exclamation points. Is it supposed to make it more fun to go to *Math!* than just *math*?

I flick the paper with my fingers and there is a *thwack* sound in the silence of the room. The *thwack* brings me back to myself and I am okay. It's like I just slipped out of the frame for a minute but now I'm back. I'm okay. There is a clock ticking. The empty sound of people's absence.

"Hey, Stacey," I say. Her chair is empty, at a half-spin, like it just propelled her out the door. I fold the paper into a plane. You have to check in with Stacey when you're late or else risk the wrath of Mr. V. I know the drill. I've always been late. Before. Then. Now.

I've never really given a fuck, to be honest.

"STACEY," I say, louder.

Someone clears her throat and I turn around. And she is there. Her.

Not Stacey.

My girl. My *imaginary* girl.

The Girl.

The room twists and heaves.

I say something. It's probably, "No way." Then I choke on nothing, really choke, an I-need-a-Heimlich kind of choke. For a second I totally can't breathe. The air clusters in my throat like clay and hardens. I gasp. No air.

Panic.

Then my lungs right themselves.

The pink paper in my hand is shaking. *Dex Pratt! Math!*

The girl has blond hair, wavy, like she's just been surfing. Skin so white it looks like porcelain. Same glasses as me. The girl who can't possibly even exist smiles at me, and even her teeth are exactly as I had pictured.

I nod at this imaginary girl and say, "Hey." Just to see if my voice is working or if this is one of those dreams where you can't speak, can't move, eventually die at the hands of an ax murderer or a doll with a chainsaw.

My voice sounds normal. I move my legs. Also normal. I guess I'm crazy then. I don't know what to do with that. I jump up on the balls of my feet and look behind me. Where is *Stacey*?

"You got what you need there, Dex?" Stacey says. I didn't see her come in. She's looking at me like she'd like to eat me, and pounces into her chair, which squeaks in protest. Stacey is an eyeful. Not in a good way. In a leopard-print-cardigan-over-leggings way. She licks her lips, which are a shade of bluish metallic pink that shouldn't exist. Her tongue makes me think of sea cucumbers. "You're muddy!" she says, like this is a good thing.

"Got it. Thanks much," I say, just as she's saying, "You're late, Dexter Pratt."

The hair on the back of my neck is prickling. I pretend it isn't. I scratch my neck hard with my nails. I can't say to Stacey, "Hey, so I'm hallucinating the girl in that green chair in the corner and I'm completely freaking out here." My brain sends me a random electrical jolt that shoots down my spine. Which is fine; I understand that, at least. It's a symptom of coming off the antidepressants that I've been taking for a while. My doctor calls it a brainstorm.

I like how that sounds.

"Just put that I had to help my dad," I tell Stacey, for the record. I shrug. "Put that down for every day, probably."

"Sure, sweetie," she says. Her eyes never once drift over to the girl in the corner.

So she *is* a hallucination.

A side effect.

She couldn't be there.

She isn't there.

That's okay then. I take a deep breath in and hold it, like toking an imaginary fattie. Hold your breath. There. It's all good. It's fine.

Safe.

Stacey slowly pulls out the ledger to write my excuse down. She writes with her left hand in a fist, like a kindergartner struggling with chalk. While she writes, she says, "How *is* your dad?" Her pen makes a horrible scratching noise on the paper. The hairs on my arms stand up.

I shrug and go, "Same old."

She smiles and says, "He's such a survivor." There's lipstick on her teeth. I can picture her applying that ugly lipstick in the rearview mirror of her car, and it makes me fucking sad, that's what it does. I know she's faking herself too. She's just a character. We're *all* just characters.

I swallow hard. "Yeah," I say. "I guess."

"Oh, he is," she says. "He really is."

I shrug because is it supposed to be heroic when you survive a jump you made by choice? I mean, come on. Give me a break. Maybe if you half died to cure cancer, people should be nice about it. But a failed suicide attempt doesn't warrant applause.

Not from me anyway.

"Good summer?" she says.

I shrug again. "Good enough," I say. I don't ask about hers. I don't care about hers. Besides, the weather outside makes summer seem like it's been gone long enough to be forgotten.

Mr. Vermillion stomps into the room, looking furious and distracted like he always does. Last night's bourbon stinking up the room as effectively as a spray can of Febreze shooting you right in the face. His belly peeks out between the pulling buttons on his shirt. "Pratt," he says, like saying my first name is far too much trouble. "Pratt, you gonna win this season?"

"I guess," I say. "Not up to me, man. It's the whole team."

"You in shape?" he says.

"Sure am," I say like I care about basketball, which I don't. I lift my shirt and thump my abdomen. He stares.

"Huh," he says. The veins in his cheeks look like failure. You just know he never wanted to end up here. And now he drinks this whole fucking depressing town away every night on his sagging couch, jerking off to porn and imagining a different life. That's the thing about this place: it stinks of failure.

It's rife with it.

You cannot get away from the smell.

No one, not one person—not Stacey, not Mr. V, not *anyone*—came here because they succeeded, because their dreams came true.

My dream is sitting in the corner on a green vinyl chair.

I keep my eyes on Mr. V and away from the girl who is clearing her throat so much I wonder if she isn't having some kind of asthma attack. I glance back. She pushes her blond hair out of her face and I swear to God I nearly faint. She smells like some kind of coconut soap and a candle that's melting. Why can I smell her? She's too far away. Can you have smell hallucinations? I must stink. I have to go to class, but my legs don't seem to want to take me. We are all just standing there like actors waiting for our cues.

This is not real.

"Pratt," says Mr. Vermillion, "show Olivia where your homeroom is. You two are later than shit."

"Nice, Mr. V," I say. I think for a second about Mr. McAllum, Head of St. Joe's. He would never say, "Later than shit." He would never say "shit." He probably doesn't even shit. He would…

Fuck it, who cares? St. Joe's may as well be the moon or a movie or something that I dreamed. See, right now my old friends there are all piling into the gym for the annual first-day-assembly, ties flapping, shirts untucked, comparing summer vacations in Europe with those spent on the boat. The life I borrowed for a while. The life I thought was one thing but turned out to be another.

I instinctively press on the bend in my elbow. Where Feral stuck that first needle into his own arm, I have a tattoo of a nautical star. It was Feral's idea. His meant something else. Mine doesn't mean anything to anyone but me. It's so small it looks like a cancerous mole. A spiky black mark.

A target.

Olivia is standing behind me. I can feel her as much as see her.

"We have the same glasses," she says. Even her voice is what I'd imagined, no joke.

"Uh-huh," I say. I am aware of how I smell—like sweat, so much sweat, and weed and my dad's Old Spice deodorant. The ass of my jeans is drenched and clammy. The mud makes me look like I've been smeared in shit, and let's face it, farm mud *is* mostly shit, so I have been.

My sneakers make a high-pitched fart on the lino floor. The sun is coming out, and for a second I lose her in the wet glare from the window. I catch a glimpse of a rainbow.

Olivia laughs, a strange high sound that makes me think of bats. She nudges me. The place where she touches me feels like something small has landed on me with cold feet. But not in a bad way, in a good one, like when you find the cool spot on the sheets with your foot and your body soaks that up and for a few seconds you feel okay.

I am dizzy in the kind of way that you are when you drink too much. I hate that feeling.

Mr. V is saying something, but I can't hear him because my ears feel funny. I brace myself against the doorjamb. The girl's teeth have a small space between them. She has four freckles on her cheek.

"I directed those," I almost say. "I did that."

"Yeah," I say instead. "Let's go. I'll show you." My voice sounds strange and tinny, like it is coming to my own ears across a long, impossible distance.

"Good day!" Stacey chirps. "First day of your last year!"

"So," Olivia says. She has a faint accent that makes me think of Africa. We climb stairs that are red linoleum criss-crossed with diamonds, which are meant to give your feet something to grip. For a second, the "so" sounds slowed down, like something melting. "So," she starts again, "you're Dex."

"Yeah," I say. "I am." I cough, and the sound is too loud. She seems to flinch or flicker, I'm not sure which.

"Have you, um, always gone to this school?" she asks.

"Yeah," I say. "It's the only school. Here. I mean, there are other schools obviously. All over the world. Millions. But just this one, here." I am not making sense. I squint. The hall seems to be stretching away from us, a million miles long. I sneak another look at the girl...this girl.

She is wearing jeans that are tight all the way to her ankles, but instead of looking like a slut, she looks like she's, I don't know, on a catwalk or something. She makes Glass look ordinary, and no one, not ever, said Glass was plain. But while Glass glittered, Olivia *gleams*.

She is more naked in those jeans than anyone I've ever seen, including naked people, if you know what I mean. Her jacket is oversize and looks military. Something pale-colored is underneath that shimmers and demands to be touched. Looking right at her hurts my eyes. And, let's face it, my dick. I keep my eyes averted, away from the shiny thing she's wearing, away from the shiny thing that she is.

Imagine walking down a long hallway with your fantasy. I am tripping bad. My mouth is so dry now that it hurts, it's cracking. Bleeding. I taste tin. I press my fingers again and again on my tattoo, like it's a button that can help me escape.

The lockers are multiplying in the corner of my eyes. Rows and rows of puke-green lockers. The floor is red lino. Our school is decorated like innards.

Our voices echo. "If you had a choice," she says. "Where would you go?"

I shrug. "Doesn't matter. School is school." I think about St. Joe's. Different. School is not just school. I am lying. I want to stop talking. My voice is bothering me, like feedback from a speaker. "Maybe I'd go to..." I shake my head. "It's high school. Who cares?"

"Well, *I'd* choose a school in New York," she says. "Like a dramatic arts school. Something other. Something...you know. Different."

It's like I put the words in her mouth, wrote them down on white paper, and now they are hanging over her head in cartoon speech bubbles, bubbles that drift like kites down the endless hall. "New York," they say. "The Himalayas." "My guitar." "Acting or modeling." I stop, stock still. I can't move. I can feel sweat trickling down my forehead.

"This kind of school is so...," she says. "I kind of hate my dad for making us come here. It feels so...predictable or something." She shudders or she doesn't, and then flips her hair around her head in a swirl that looks like something moving down a drain.

"Yeah," I say. "I knew you'd say that."

"How do you know?" she says.

"I don't," I say. "But I bet I know what you'd say about a lot of things. Like I bet you're a vegetarian, right? I bet you play the guitar and sing. I bet...well. I don't want to bet.

I think I know you. I don't want to sound crazy, but you..." I am talking too fast. I can see her face, just out of focus, looking at my quizzically. "I guess I just know your type," I finish. "Anyway, we're here. This is it. Our classroom. Homeroom. Whatever."

The door to the classroom is liver brown. Someone has written on it with a black pen, *RUN FOR YOUR LIFE*. She touches the words with her finger. Her nails are pale pink but also bitten to the quick, and she hides them when she notices me noticing.

I didn't give her bitten nails. I relax a little.

Then the door swings open and Tanis rushes out. "Bathroom!" she says, seeing me, but she stops to grab me, hug me, I guess, and I'm not ready for it. For her. I fall on the floor, hard, smashing my funny bone and pushing her off at the same time, and when I look up again, Olivia has vanished and Tanis is laughing, sitting on me.

"I really have to pee!" she says.

And Mrs. Singh is saying, "That's enough. Tanis and Dex stop it right now or you'll be in detention for the rest of your lives." She looks down, disgusted. "You aren't puppies, you know," she adds, sighing.

"Woof," says Tanis. She gets up in one movement. There is something about Tanis that is ridiculously bendy. She makes me think of a noodle. She runs down the hall.

I try to smile because that is what a normal kid would do when his hot girlfriend jumps him in the hallway, right? I try to look sheepish maybe, or proud, and then I give up on trying to look anything and get to my feet. I slide into my seat in time for the bell to ring and for T-dot to smack me in the head and pull me away into a conversation about the team and the coach and a new guy named Phil Stars who is six foot six or ten or something. And when I look around, I'm in the crowd in the big fat pulsing blue vein of the hallway, and it's like Olivia doesn't even exist.

"Right?" says T-dot.

"Yeah," I go. "Totally."

He nods, like I've said something smart. Punches a locker. He's only five foot nine, but he's wide and tough, more like a football guy than a basketball guy, but he's better than you'd expect.

"Can't wait," he says. He is made entirely out of muscle, which somehow makes him rubbery. He's always bouncing up and down. He can't hold still.

I can't honestly remember why we call him T-dot. I think his real name is Todd or Tad or some fucking thing, but I can't really remember that either. I want to ask him, but he'd probably be totally insulted that I—his best friend—can't remember his actual name, so I bite my tongue.

T-dot is a swimmer, which means that his hair is always wet and he always smells like the community pool. No one here thinks of swimming as a "real" sport. They think it's lame. But T-dot doesn't really care what other people think. He's also on every single team in the school because he's good at every single sport. You can't really call the quarterback lame just because he's also a swimmer.

He whoops for no reason.

"What?" I say.

"I'm PUMPED!" he says. "Man, I've missed this shithole. Basketball, here we COME!"

"Settle down," I say.

"Can't," he says. "You're excited, admit it."

"Yeah, sure," I tell him.

"Arooooo!" he howls like a wolf. Everything about T-dot is normal and not normal. He's more himself than anyone I know. I am jealous of that. But not of him. Jackson Barry leaps by and grabs T into a headlock, and for a few seconds they bang off the lockers before collapsing, out of breath.

"Dude," says T-dot.

"Dude," says Jackson.

I want to say "Dude" too, but if I said it, it would sound forced, so I don't say anything. Instead I scan the crowd for Olivia, but she is not there. Not anywhere.

My brain jolts again, the electricity of it trickling down my spine. Tanis leans on my arm, back from the bathroom, I guess. She is frantically texting and holding her breath while she types. She can type with one hand faster than anyone I know.

"There," she says. Like a text to Kate is an accomplishment. She's chewing gum and it's making a crackling sound and I want to run, but I don't, because I have Math! next and going to class is all part of this normal-guy fakery that I'm working on.

"How's Kate?" I say.

"She's good," says Tanis. "Do you care?"

"Yeah," I say. "No. Whatever."

Kate has never liked me, which makes Kate smarter than most people. She thinks I hate her because she's fat but she's wrong. I hate her because I think she can see through me to my rotten core. Kate loves Tanis. There's nothing wrong with that. Someone should. I get this creepy feeling that Kate can see exactly how much I love Tanis and has judged it to be not enough. Which it isn't, because I think love is a mindfuck and I'm not going to play, because it's the kind of game that ends up with you naked on the top of a grain elevator and your dog barking at the bottom. Kate hates me and she should.

Tanis works her hand into my pocket. Her hand is tiny. Her nails are perfect, each one painted with a pattern that

I happen to know is hieroglyphics because Tanis is obsessed with that shit.

What girl has hieroglyphics on her nails?

There is a lot to love about Tanis.

For example, she's a genius. You wouldn't know it to look at her. You'd think she was kind of slutty, kind of weird, kind of tough. She's got the look of someone who would scratch your eyes out given half the chance.

But she wouldn't.

She may be glaring at you, but probably she's not even seeing you, she's seeing something else. Numbers, most likely.

Ratios.

Patterns.

Proportions.

I can't really explain what it is because I have *no* idea. Math and I are mortal enemies, but Tanis is like this mathematician-artist freak. She does stuff with math. She makes it into art. I'm not explaining it well, mostly because I don't understand it. I'm pretty fucking stupid in a lot of ways.

She wants to be a model, right? But she's borderline too-short, and there's the thing of her face being half normal and half frozen, some family trait with a name I've forgotten. But she's a girl who does what she wants and then figures everything out, so she's studied all these models—her bedroom walls are papered with magazine pictures of gorgeous models, and on each one she has listed their proportions. Leg length to torso. Head size to hips. Like somewhere in there is a magical formula, which actually she says there is and if she can grow two more inches of legs, she'll have it all in the right proportions, which I believe because she really does have a fucking incredible body.

You wouldn't guess to look at her that she'd ever analyze anything that closely. That she'd know how to do statistical analysis of breast size. Or that she'd want to.

Or that she's wrong, because in Tanis's case, her perfect proportions don't mean jack because of her *face*.

Anyway, her dad is mentally challenged and her mom is gone and her life is as shitty as mine when you look at it up close, which I try not to do because I have enough problems, right? But then she measures something and calculates something and draws it, and *bam*, it's in its place. She has control. The numbers and patterns and all that crap, it makes her feel okay, so whatever.

Good for her.

Tanis is a perfect girlfriend. She never asks too much. She never wants to "just talk." She's just weird enough to be interesting. And she thinks she's in love with me.

She thinks she knows who I am.

As *if*.

Right now her curly hair is hanging forward over her face and she really is killer sexy, even her crookedness is hot, so why do I hate her right now? Her hand is in my pocket, rubbing in a circle, and I push it away.

"Hey," she says.

"Gotta have a slash," I mumble and dart into the boys. I sit down on a toilet and try to feel sane, which fails. On the wall in the washroom it says, *FOR A HOT HAND JOB, CALL TANIS B.* I try to rub it out with toilet paper, but it's permanent ink. I scratch at it with a ballpoint and then give up. The number is wrong anyway.

Mr. V is a pedophile, the wall says.

And *FUCK YO MOMMA.*

The walls are this really pale shade of mucous yellow, and even though it's the first day of school, the bathroom stinks of sewage. I press my cheek against the cold metal just for a minute and close my eyes and remind myself that this is easy.

School is the easiest place to be.

So why am I so freaked out?

Olivia couldn't possibly exist in a place like this.

She doesn't, right?

I mean, how can she?

chapter 7

By Christmas of last year, Feral was in rehab, Dad was out of rehab, I had moved back to Hell and my life was shit.

The Christmas before that, I was in Vancouver and the silver tree was nearly hidden behind a mountain of presents.

It's like a game of Spot the Differences, made easier by the fact that everything was different.

I haven't talked about Feral much. Not yet. He's my brother. My stepbrother. Feral is a heroin addict. "Recovering," they said. We were to call him a "recovering addict." Frank the Recovering Addict.

Fuck that. He was Feral and always would be.

When I moved, I didn't tell him. He was "working through his issues" and apparently his issues included me. I wasn't allowed to see him, speak to him or contact him.

SD seemed to think that all of it was my fault. That Feral's addiction had something to do with me.

My mom agreed.

My own fucking mom *agreed*.

I wanted to argue. I wanted to scream. I wanted to do a lot of things that I didn't do. Smash things. I wanted to smash glass. All the glass. Everything. I wanted Feral back. I wanted I wanted I wanted, and no one fucking cared.

Feral was the alpha, no doubt about it. I would have followed him anywhere. I did follow him everywhere. He was FERAL. I was just Feral's stepbrother.

Without Feral, I was nobody.

I tried to tell them, but no one was listening.

Feral's addiction erased me.

The thinner he got and the more strung out, the less anyone cared what I was saying. Even Feral started to squint at me while I was talking, like he couldn't quite remember who I was. We still did shit—played our crappy music, hung out—but he was mostly gone. Just gone. At school, I started to fade. Without him next to me, kids talked through me. Past me. Even Glass started to drift. She was still with me, but I could tell she was gone.

I needed Feral.

We did everything together. Every. Fucking. Thing.

And he left me and I was alone and I stopped caring about everything. I know how that sounds.

And I know that it's true.

And when school started again that fall, St. Joe's without Feral was stupid. And he bounced in and out of rehab like neither place could hold on to him. I stopped talking. No one noticed. I started making movies every day, miles of movies, more and more movies. And I wasn't talking—why didn't anyone notice? Or care?

I was making a documentary. "The Disappearance of Dex Pratt" it was called. Then I changed it to "The Invisible Dex." Then I changed it back.

Then I deleted it.

Then I dragged it out of the trash and saved it in a file called *Fuck You*.

Then it was November and my dad was out of rehab, and I was being called home. Imagine there were trumpets. There weren't, but if you imagine them, it's more dramatic. In real life, there were just a bunch of phone calls and "arrangements" and the strange set of my mom's lips when she said, "You should go."

The gray hairs that freckled her haircut like lines of disappointment.

The way her hand shook when she reached for the milk.

SD said, "It's not your fault." He said that. SD is a big guy. When he hugged me, I could hardly breathe. But I didn't believe him. He thought it was my fault. I know he thought that because he gave me a check. The number of zeroes on it said, "I feel guilty for blaming you for all of this shit, but I *do*." I'm not stupid. I know how it works.

I put the money in the bank. "For college."

Yeah, right.

I was glad to leave that glass house. I would have been gladder to blow it up, watch all that glass fall down on the city like diamonds or snow. I don't know if I told you about the house. The way it splayed out over the cliff and the wall of glass made it so that any room you were in allowed you to see the whole glittering city below you. Feral used to say that when we flushed the toilets, it rained on the people. "The people." Like we were not included.

Feral was kind of an asshole that way. Entitled prick. Doesn't mean I didn't love him, just means I could see what he was like.

I used to think that it was like living in a fish tank with everyone down below staring up into our windows, watching us swim from room to room, blowing bubbles as we went. But by the time I moved out, it was still like that, only I'd forgotten how to breathe underwater and every inhalation was like drowning.

Every time I think about Feral, I lie. I am lying right now.

I am lying. I am a liar.

I have a tattoo on the inside of my arm. It was my idea. It wasn't even an idea. It was a thing that I did. I thought it was cool. I *am* the one.

It was me.

I drowned, but Feral died.

See, I could do heroin for fun, once or twice. It didn't matter. He couldn't. Some people are like that. From the very first time, it owned him, creeping through his veins like mercury, turning him into a robot who existed only for more.

And Feral, he was gone.

And I was "home." But it wasn't my home.

And Vancouver wasn't my home.

The truth was, I was only "home" when I was behind my camera. And without it, I was too light, like any minute I might just float up into the sky and never come down. I saw the whole world through that lens; it kept me just far enough away to be safe. And now that it was gone, it was like looking at everything through binoculars. The world was too big and there was too much of it.

It didn't help that this shitty town felt like a sweater I'd outgrown years ago that I was trying to pull back on and it wasn't working. It itched and I don't think it was really ever my sweater, ever. I never would have chosen it.

In March, I lost Feral.

In June, my dad jumped.

In September, I began disappearing.

In December, I moved back and started over. As someone else. Another Dex. If I still had the camera, I'd be filming "The Evolution of Dex Pratt." Or "The Rebirth." Only, that sounds good, and there was nothing good about this.

And then there was the house. My dad thought it was *genius*. I couldn't argue with him even though there were lots of good, decent arguments. I just didn't have any left. And I wanted some drugs, something, anything to shut out all the noise. And that was the fucking irony because I wanted and I wanted and I wanted, but I didn't mean...

You know how they say, "Be careful what you wish for?" Yeah, it was like that.

Anyway, even broken, my dad was not someone you argued with.

Even in the pictures in the ad, the house looked like the kind of house where you end up. Not one that you choose. It was not the kind of house where the Dad that I thought I knew would ever live. Where were the polished wood floors and the fucking stainless steel appliances? Where was all the *stuff*? Soaker tubs and a front lawn? A deck?

"It has a perfect basement," he said. "Think about it. It's on a working farm so no one will question the power use, and it has a huge basement. It's perfect."

This was the New, Improved Dad™.

The New, Improved Dad™ had had it. He'd had enough lawyering, he said, for ten lifetimes. The dealers made the money and ran, and he made shit and stayed. And now he was going to rake it in. He knew people. He knew everyone. He knew loopholes. It was like his whole life had been building up to this decision and he was going to fucking go for it whether or not it cost him everything. Because he had nothing left to lose.

And now it was his *turn*. And, oh, by the way, son, all that hydroponic equipment from the old house is about to be very, very handy.

"Our Joe is a psychopath," I said flatly. "This is a nightmare."

"I know Our Joe," said Dad. I stared at him.

Everyone knew Our Joe, like you know the bad guy in every town. Rich as fuck and always doing things like riding his bike into town naked and handing flowers to "the ladies." Then the next day sending the newspaper letters about how the government was affecting our minds through radio waves, and the next burning down his neighbor's barn. He was the guy who you'd guess would end up with bodies in the basement or at least a mysteriously dismembered dog. He was Stephen King–creepy, but this wasn't Maine, or a novel. This was our life.

He was one tinfoil hat short of an insane asylum, one more crime away from jail, and living on his land sounded about as good an idea as rooming with a werewolf.

Never mind that the house he was renting out was pretty much appropriate only for the set of a horror movie.

"Yeah," I said finally. "You know him. So why are we moving in with him?"

"We're not." He laughed. "We're renting a house on his property. Don't be so stupid. It works and you know it."

I thought about how, when my sister and I were little, Dad made us cross the street when Our Joe was coming. I thought about how Mom flinched and screamed when he knocked on our car window once to offer her a half-dead flower, grinning enough to reveal the gaps between his silver teeth. How she stomped on the gas and squealed away.

The thing with Our Joe was that, from a certain angle, he looked like a kindly old man. But everyone knew that he wasn't.

Just knew. Like how dogs always know when you're scared.

Everyone knew, that is, except him. He thought he was charming, you could tell. He thought he was "fun."

Crazy fucker.

So then we were driving toward Our Joe's cornfields, lurching and sliding this way and that in the snow, narrowly missing the ditch so many times that I thought we'd both be in wheelchairs before long.

Dad didn't seem to notice, he was rambling on about our new "life." The car stank of stale cigarette smoke even though neither of us smoked. I felt sick from that smell. I felt like the smell was in my throat, choking me.

"We're going to make a killing," Dad said.

I wanted to grab him and say, "What the FUCK, Dad? What are you SAYING?" But there was a ringing in my ears, and my eyes kept blurring. I kept thinking of the time he taught me to swim in the lake down the road. Like that's anything to do with anything, but it's what I thought about. How he stood there waist-deep in the lake for what felt like the entire summer with mosquitoes biting a belt around his waist. The water was not quite clear, and through the silty screen my feet looked a million miles away. I kept pushing off because he told me to, letting go of the ground with my feet. And each time I'd float for a second, and then I'd stop.

I sank and I sank and I sank and cried a million times. I remember crying. Snot bubbles. The whole works. But he wouldn't let me quit. T-dot would swim by like a goddamn mermaid, and I just couldn't do it and couldn't do it. My dad kept waiting and trying and showing me again, and suddenly I could do it. I did do it. I took in great mouthfuls of that filthy water, which I could taste in my nose for days, but I did it. I splashed along for a few strokes and I stopped crying and I didn't drown, and my dad said, "There." Like that was that. The end of swimming lessons.

I guess a good end to that story would be that I turned into an Olympic swimmer but I didn't. At least I know how not to drown. But in that Volkswagen with the heat blasting on that freezing cold day, driving toward "home," listening to my dad talking about different strains of marijuana, drowning was exactly what I was doing. All that was missing was the snot bubbles.

"It's a plant," Dad added, like that clarified everything. "Anyway, fuck it. Fuck the system. Fuck it all."

"Dad," I said. But didn't know really what to say. When my dad said "fuck," it stung. He kept saying it. It's all I could hear. *Fuck, fuck, fuck*. Here's your fucking childhood, and fuck it. I was dizzy with images. Dad reading me bedtime stories. Dad pretending to be Santa Claus for the school Christmas party. Dad laughing, bent over by the side of the road while I rode by on my bike. Dad smiling, Dad talking, Dad not fucking swearing. *Fuck*, *fuck*, *fuck*. He kept talking.

I felt like I was being swarmed by wasps. I needed him to stop. I had to concentrate on the road. A brown deer suddenly darted out in front of the car and stopped, stock still, in my path. I slammed on the brakes, swearing. The swerve spun us in a whole slow-motion circle. My heartbeat swirled. I held my breath. The deer stared and then took off.

"Be careful," Dad said mildly when we finally stopped, still pointing in the direction we were going in the first place. "Try not to kill us."

"That's fucking ironic," I muttered, but I'm pretty sure he didn't hear me.

And then we were there, and it was worse than I thought, and it was home.

I was surprised how quickly my friends came back to me.

T-dot, at least. He was there the day we moved in, just sitting there on the front stoop like that was a totally normal thing to do. Waiting to help me move like I was moving into a college dorm or something.

That was T-dot. Big grin like it was a Welcome Home party and not as entirely messed up as it was. When we were kids, we'd egg this house on Halloween. This exact house. It was as close as we had to a haunted house in our town, and besides, Our Joe's presence made it scary enough. We used to toilet paper the front porch. No one had lived here, ever, as far as I knew, except Our Joe and his wife, back in the day.

It was snowing lightly and snow was stuck in T-dot's hair. The white dusting on the house made it look pretty from a distance, but from up close, it looked like a clapboard catastrophe, like a place where squatters would smoke crack or a house where someone had died ten years before and no one had noticed.

"Dude," T-dot said. He clapped me on the shoulder, hard enough that my skin hurt through my ski jacket.

"What's up?" I said. "Don't have anything better to do than hang around this dump? It isn't Halloween, you know." Embarrassingly, my voice kind of caught, like a stuck zipper. He pretended not to notice. I stared at him with cold eyes, daring him to say something about the house, about me, about the whole fucking mess that it was, but he didn't.

He grinned.

I laughed. It felt weird. I hadn't laughed for a long time. And then we were both laughing, hitting each other, but not really. Doing that thing where you wrestle but maybe it's a hug, but it's not. And then we're lying in the snow-covered dirt, him all wholesome white teeth and wet hair from the pool, and me too skinny and wild-eyed and given up for dead, laughing in the snow.

"Oh, man," he said. "Where have you been? I totally missed you."

"Yeah," I said. "Well, I was in Vancouver." That was the truth, but there was more that I couldn't say. That he wouldn't understand. T-dot had never once stuck something in his arm. Never once smoked anything. Never once left himself, twirled around the universe and came back fucked in the head.

"I know it," he said. "Vancouver's awesome."

"Yeah," I said. "Good to see you too."

We lay there and watched it snow for a while. It wasn't long ago that we would have *played* in the goddamned snow. Now we just looked at it.

"Snow sucks," he said.

"Yeah," I said. Moving was shitty enough without slipping on the steps. I wanted so much in that moment to go back to the me that would have thrown a snowball or written my name in the snow with piss or something. I felt like I could practically reach out and grab that part of myself, but there was glass in between the two of us, or ice, and then the moment passed and it was too late.

"We better do it now," I said. "It's only going to get worse. I can't believe this fucking weather."

"Yeah," he said, but he was grinning. We got up. He kicked some snow into a little pile. Bent down and rolled it into a ball. Threw it hard against the mailbox, where it exploded like a hand grenade. Ice flying through the air.

"Score," I said.

We dusted ourselves off and slowly unloaded the U-Haul that Dad had packed all those months before. Everything was dirty. I don't know how it got so dirty.

We didn't talk much, except when the couch slipped out of our hands and fell hard, upside down, the underside issuing up a giant belch of dust, and we fought to right it just as the snow turned thick and started to fall for real.

"Never thought you'd be back, dude," said T-dot.

"Never thought I would be either," I said. I was sweating. My breath steamed hot against the falling flakes.

"Dex?" he said. "Sorry about your dad."

"Well, *you* didn't do it," I said. I noticed he was sweating too. Red-faced. There was a lump in my throat. I wasn't going to goddamn *cry*. "Everyone's sorry," I added. "Especially me."

"Sure," he said. "I just meant...nah, forget it."

I shrugged. Pretended there was something in my eye.

I didn't know what I was supposed to do. Tell him everything? Nothing? Pretend it was all normal?

In the end, that's what I went with: Pretending.

I never told him about Feral.

In return, T-dot didn't tell me what I missed. I figured I knew. Enough anyway.

We shoved the furniture around in the rooms. In the end, we had all this extra junk: My little sister Chelsea's bedroom stuff. The bed that was in the guest room at our old house. Mom's old desk. Two couches and nowhere to put them. A TV the size of a fireplace.

"I'll dump them," offered T-dot.

"Thanks," I said. "Let's just shove them downstairs." I was exhausted. My entire body hurt. But it was done. The work was done. I was home. I shook T-dot's hand. "Thanks," I said. "Really. I totally couldn't have done this alone."

"Hey," he said, "forget it."

I drove him back home. T-dot lived down at the bottom of the valley in a "new" subdivision that was twenty years old. His house was all lit up with Christmas lights and a fake Santa on the lawn that waved and spun. It looked so *normal.* My mouth filled with acid. It was something about how the windows glowed in the falling snow. I guessed that our windows would glow too, but somehow it wouldn't be the same. I bet his family still had a family *game* night.

"See you," he said.

"Tell your mom and dad 'hi,'" I said. I wanted him to invite me in. I wanted hot chocolate and *SpongeBob* movies, just like when we were kids. I wanted.

But whatever.

"Yeah," he said. "Will do." He didn't mention my dad.

As soon as he got out, I wished I'd said more. I needed to talk to someone. I needed it bad. I had never felt so fucking alone.

Never.

Enter Tanis, stage right. Or left. Or wherever.

Tanis Bowerman.

I'd known her my whole life, but I'd never paid much attention to her. I don't know why.

But there she was, behind the till at the Safeway I stopped at on the way back to the motel where Dad was watching TV or mapping out our future with a Bic pen and a yellow legal pad. Calculating. Waiting.

I had dried sweat itching all over me, and the cold made it worse. I felt like my entire head was chapped. I wanted something, but I wasn't going to find it at Safeway. I felt like I was hopping under my skin. I wanted.

I wanted.

I grabbed some chips and soda, a bag of apples, my dad's favorite tea.

Tanis rang in my stuff. Then she looked me slowly up and down, and she said, "Dexter Fuckin' Pratt. Slumming, are you?"

"Fuck you, Tanis," I said automatically. She had the most bizarre-colored eyes. Gray, I guess, but they looked silver. One big, the other much smaller, or maybe they just seemed that way because of the way her face was. Everything about her made me think of shadows.

"Hey," she said. She bit her lip, and I almost threw myself over the counter to kiss it. It was like that. Instant. Like I didn't have a choice. Like a brainstorm, only this one came from somewhere in my pants. I shuddered.

"Sorry," she said.

"Whatever." I shrugged. "When are you off?"

I'm not that guy. I don't *talk* like that. I'm not him. I have a girlfriend. Had a girlfriend. Then. I still talked to Glass every day, even though she'd already done the "seeing other people" speech (the day after I left). I was still hoping. And she'd already mostly stopped answering my calls.

In seven days.

The truth was that Glass wasn't the kind of person who wanted to be needed. She wasn't that kind of girlfriend. She was the kind of girlfriend who appreciated the amount of camera time I gave her. She was the kind of girlfriend who thought I was going to be famous one day. She was the kind of girlfriend who was smart enough to see when someone was about to bottom out and to get out of the way. She was the kind of girlfriend who made drugs look pretty.

Fuck her.

Tanis was still staring at me. "Are you going to pay me or just stand there and stare?" she said.

"Uh," I said. 'Cause I'm smooth like that. She tucked her hair behind her ear. It was so shiny, it looked like it had been oiled. Coils of it. Medusa snakes. The thing with Tanis. Well.

I couldn't figure out why I'd never noticed her before.

Before I moved away, Tanis and I hadn't exactly been in the same social circle, if you know what I mean. She was a skid. I wasn't. If you think of us as bars of soap, I was Ivory and she was the cheap kind that slipped off your skin before cleaning it. Hard, and carved into some kind of shape, like a fish or a golf club.

But she was hot. Tanis was always hot.

And I wanted to fall into her crooked face. I wanted to lick it. I didn't know what was wrong with me. I felt like a dog in heat. I held out my money and she took it.

"Ten," she said. "I'm off at ten."

It was only nine. I didn't go anywhere. I sat in the car and ate three apples. The way they crunched and dripped when I ate them was weirdly satisfying. I drank a soda.

I nearly froze to death.

I was waiting for her outside the front door of the Safeway at exactly ten, standing on the sidewalk covered with flattened chewed gum and cigarette butts and a thin layer of frost where the snow had been plowed off.

The chewed gum under that ice made me think of fish frozen into the lake. Which made me think about me frozen into the lake. I could almost see myself, under my own feet. A chalk outline under the ice.

I shook my head. Rubbed my eyes. “Stop it,” I said.

It was dark and so cold that my hands turned blue. I didn’t care. Tanis came out. She walked like she was nervous, too straight, like she was being judged. She kept touching her hair. We kissed right away, fast and hard, our teeth jarring and crashing, like we were drunk and hooking up at a party in someone’s parents’ basement. But we weren’t drunk and it wasn’t a party.

“What was *that*?” she said, pulling away.

“I couldn’t help it,” I said. “I was just…well…”

“What?” she said.

“I think I was looking for you,” I said.

“You don’t know what you’re talking about,” she said. “You’re just horny.”

“I’m not,” I lied. “I mean, I am now. Who says ‘horny’?”

She was laughing. Her teeth were narrow and a bit too long. She had a dimple high up in her right cheek. I wanted to stop noticing things. I sort of wanted to consume her.

“You really have changed, Dex Pratt,” she said. “I guess we have to talk first, maybe, huh?”

"Not if you don't want to," I said. Her lips were pink, but it couldn't have been lipstick. That would have been gone by now. I stared at her mouth.

"But," she said, "I do."

It wasn't like in the movies. We didn't sit down right there and share everything. I had to go. Dad would be worried. She was laughing, like this all was the funniest thing in the world. And maybe it was. Or she was laughing *at* me. I couldn't tell. I didn't care. I felt like something had tilted and I was just scrambling to stay on it. She picked up a handful of snow and threw it at me. If I'd been myself, I would have thrown it back or blocked it, but I didn't and it hit me square in the nose. A block of ice. My nostril dripped blood.

"Fuck," I said.

"Oh my god," she said. "I'm so sorry."

"I've got to go," I said. "I'll see you."

Back then, I couldn't leave my dad alone for long. That was before we had extra help. I was *everything*. And the whole time I was worried that he was doing something. That he'd do something. Something crazy.

I didn't trust him yet.

"Wait," she said. "You can't do that, you jerk. You can't come here and kiss me and run off."

"I have to," I said. "My dad…" My nose spattered blood onto the white snow. We both looked at it. It looked like one of those shapes you're supposed to interpret and that tells you something about your personality. I thought it looked like a blood splatter on snow.

"Looks like poodles dancing," she said. "Those things always look like poodles to me."

"What?" I laughed. The laugh felt funny, like I was going to be sick. Maybe it was just blood on my gag reflex.

"Oh," she said. She was going to say something else, but I stopped her by walking away. That's how it was with us. She was always wanting to say something more and I was always leaving.

I got back to the motel and Dad was asleep in his chair. He was all slumped over. He looked so old. I never fucking cried except for then, when he was asleep and couldn't hear me. For a second, I thought about killing him. Then it would be over. He'd be dead. I'd go to jail. Maybe that would be easier. Maybe then I'd know who I was.

I was just so mad. Inside, bubbling over. And so goddamn *sad*.

The TV was showing infomercials for some kind of gym equipment. The guy on the screen was bouncing an actual quarter off his own abs. I could do that, I thought. And so what?

Dad was smiling in his sleep and I couldn't even take it. The floral smell of the motel room and the way the carpet was worn in a pattern from the bed to the bathroom and the lights of the cars going by on the highway and flashing in the window every few seconds like searchlights, looking for something that was long, long gone.

The next day, we moved into the house.

I was back. There was T-dot. There was Tanis. And there and there and there and everywhere was my dad, needing me. And never once saying, "Hey, thanks."

Speaking of entitled pricks.

chapter 8
september 6, this year.

By the end of the school day, the sun is out and it is sweltering hot. The kind of hot that says there is a thunderstorm coming. The kind of hot that makes you remember that just last week—just yesterday—it was summer. Not the kind of summer you expected to have, maybe, but still summer.

The kind of hot that makes you laugh, makes things funny—T-dot doing a cartwheel in the hall, the tall new guy smacking his head on the door frame and falling backward, Mr. V's crooked toupee—even though you aren't a laughing guy anymore. It isn't really you anyway.

It's Pretend You. Fake You. The New You.

Hey, you're pretty good at this, after all.

Everyone tumbles out of the doors after school like kids younger than they are. People are always tripping to get out those doors, and the doors are always just slightly too narrow. And you can imagine that from the outside it looks like the school is vomiting kids in fits and starts, finally spitting out the last few stragglers and then leaning over, done. Spent.

Or something like that.

After school, I shoot hoops with the boys, just like we did every day last year after I suddenly arrived back in town. And they opened up and accepted me like I'd never left. Just tossed me the ball and kept playing.

Just like they probably did the year before when I wasn't there, and the year before that while I was with Feral, filming things and laughing, and with Glass, doing drugs and fucking and not necessarily laughing. I was somewhere else, being someone else, but maybe this is who I was all along.

A normal guy.

This guy. With the basketball. The sound of it being dribbled on the pavement, the slap of my hand on its skin, the metallic sound of ball hitting rim, the *thwack* of it on the backboard, the way it feels in my hand.

And I'm not going to lie. I do feel normal and I like it. I am hot. Sweating. The moisture trickling down my spine in a good way. Tanis is watching from the sidelines, leaning on her friend Kate. People are always leaning on Kate. I think I mentioned that Kate was big. She is huge. She is like a planet. Not loose, but held tightly together and just totally enormous. It doesn't help that she wears a lot of green and blue.

She's a globe.

Mother Earth.

I wonder if she does that on purpose, looks that way. And I think fleetingly—not really, I mean, I don't think I think it—that maybe I should have picked Kate. Like it would have been a choice. But still. I don't know. Tanis is so *sharp*. It's the way she's sure of everything. But she's Tanis. So.

But whatever it is, there is something totally hot about Kate.

Maybe it's just that she hates me. Maybe it's that simple.

Something we have in common.

T-dot is doing her and not telling. I didn't know this, and then I did. It fell into place today at lunch, the way she reached over and wiped some stray crumb off his shirt, and in that second, the way he looked at her, I knew.

If I'd had my camera, I'd have filmed it and showed him later. He's a better actor than he knows. In that split second, he told me everything everything everything, and I was so surprised, I choked on my chocolate milk and nearly puked on the table.

“Are you okay?” said Tanis. “Don’t die.” But while she said it, she rubbed my back.

“No,” I gasped. “Choking.”

“Mrs. D is such a bitch this year,” she said to Kate. “She hates me.”

“No, she doesn’t,” said Kate. “She hates *us*.”

“Jealous,” said Tanis. “Because we’re hot young things.”

They giggled. I looked at T-dot. He grinned and shrugged. I raised my eyebrows. Nothing.

It made me miss Feral. It made me miss him like someone physically reached into me and tore out my stomach through my skin and squeezed it. It made me text him even though I knew he wouldn’t answer because he wasn’t the kind of guy, anymore, who shared either. Couldn’t. I don’t know. Maybe he changed his number. People do.

I did.

For some reason I flashed back to the first day of school last year. We wore uniforms, white shirts, blue striped ties, gray pants. Fucking uniforms. But that morning, I wandered into Feral’s room and he was shirtless, sitting backward on his desk chair, staring at his bed. There were these two white shirts laid out, like a maid would do, but we didn’t have a maid. Perfectly laid out. They looked like the same goddamn shirt. Feral was twitching his leg up and down, jittering.

"Are you gonna get dressed or go to school naked?" I said.

"I can't decide," he said. "I can't decide." He kept saying it, staring at those shirts.

"It's the same shirt, F," I said. "Who cares?"

"They aren't the same," he said. He spun around on his chair and his face was furious, like I didn't understand anything. "They aren't the same." He tapped his foot. His hair flopped into his face. "They aren't the same," he repeated.

"Whatever," I said. I picked one up and threw it at him. "Try this one, and hurry up, asshole, or we'll be late."

He tensed; I thought he was going to hit me. There was something about the way he was looking at me, at the shirt, that I didn't understand. Feral was so...Feral. He was the one everyone followed, the one everyone wanted to be. Something was wrong and I didn't know what to do. The shirts were the same. The fucking *same*.

I walked out of the room. That's how I helped him. I turned my back, walked away. Aren't I a champ?

Tanis tapped me on the shoulder and I jumped about a mile. "What?" I said.

"You were sleeping," she said. "Or daydreaming."

"No, I wasn't," I said. Right away, flash point. I was angry at her for no reason. At least, no reason that was her fault. "Fuck off," I said. The cafeteria was too loud and bright. It was hurting my ears, my eyes, my brain.

I could see the hurt flash across her face, and then she shrugged. That's Tanis. It's like you can penetrate her wall, but just as quickly, she puts up her shields.

"Sorry," I said.

"Whatever," she said. "Be an asshole." She stuck out her tongue.

"I said sorry," I said.

"Yeah, well, wish you didn't have to," she said. She turned back to Kate and whispered something in her ear. Girls whispering. I hate that shit. Kate looked at me and smirked, and I wanted to throw my tray in her face, but I didn't.

I didn't.

I made myself smile. Teeth. Eyes. Look at me, I'm smiling, I thought. I'm not a bad guy. It's just me, Dex.

I'm okay.

"Hey," I said to Tanis. "Want to come over later?"

She shrugged. "Maybe," she said. "I hate that place. Maybe we could go somewhere else."

"Can't," I said. "Gotta be there for Dad."

"I guess," she sighed. "Let's go, Kate." They pushed back their chairs and left without a backward glance.

"Yo," I said to T-dot. "There they go."

"Yeah," he said. "It's *time* to go, Dex. Bell went."

"Oh," I said. I didn't hear it. I'm underwater and my ears are full.

Something is wrong with me. My nerve endings are all exposed to the air and breezes hurt and my eyes want to close and I want there to be water closing in over me.

I texted Tanis, *What's up with Kate and T?*

She didn't answer. I kept staring at my phone, waiting. Wasn't she supposed to tell me everything? Isn't that what girls do? T-dot drummed the table with his hands. Crumbs flew around on it like hopping fleas. I watched the crumbs. *Drum, drum.* "Gotta fly, dude," he said, darting away. The crumbs settled. I still couldn't move.

I should have known about T-dot and Kate. It should have been obvious. The way she looked at him. The way he never looked back at her unless it was late and he was sort of wasted. I'd watched it all summer and missed it. All summer.

Summer was a blur. It got hotter and then it got cooler again. Sometimes it rained and there were mosquitoes. We drove to the lake in Dad's Volkswagen and sat there for days at a time, it felt like. We must have gone home at night. We did go home at night. Except for that once.

When Tanis told me what she told me.

Didn't she know she wasn't supposed to *need* me?

Mosquitoes in the air between us, one settling on her cheek. I slapped it. Her. I slapped her. She told me this awful thing and I slapped her and I cried, and now I can't remember what it was. How fucked up is that?

I remember the mosquitoes and the way it felt like they were in our ears, the buzzing was so loud. We ate them when we talked. There were so many. My skin was red and itchy. I scratched and bled. And then we slept there, in the shack, and we woke up, naked, covered with those fucking bites like you wouldn't believe.

The thing she told me was about Our Joe. It was like a handful of shocks. Here's one and here's another. Our Joe is Tanis's grandfather.

Zap.

And there was this time. This one time. No, all the time. She stayed at the house. She lived in the house. She didn't.

I can't get it straight. What happened? I am mixing it up with something else, a movie that I saw.

Did she say what I think she said?

She showed me a scar, fat and angry. In a place where there shouldn't be a scar.

And she said he...

And he took pictures and then...

When her grandmother found out...

And then he...

And her grandmother died.

But I can't remember. I can't remember. I can remember, but it's too much because it's worse than my goddamn story, worse than any story. It's a movie I didn't want to see. I hate those fucking movies and did she say that he...?

We slept in the shack.

The next morning we were covered with bites, and Kate and T-dot were still there. Where did they sleep? There was a tent. They weren't bitten. They were happy. They were laughing. Tanis and I weren't laughing. She probably wished she hadn't said. I didn't know what to do. It was like someone threw me a ball and I didn't know what sport it was supposed to be, so I just put it down and...

We had a fire. We made a fire to cook on. No, it wasn't a fire; it was a little cookstove and there was bacon and eggs spitting in a pan. They were goddamn good eggs. And it was hot already even though we'd just got up. It was really hot, so we had beer and pot instead of coffee, and Tanis was giggling a lot, nervous. *Giggle, giggle.*

It wasn't funny. I was so mad. Why was I mad?

I can remember, but I don't want to remember. I remember that we were all there. The four of us. There was a plan.

What was the plan?

I don't know what I'm talking about. I didn't know then. I remember crying. Tanis was crying. The sex was hot.

We didn't have sex. I don't actually remember. I was high as a fucking kite.

She shouldn't tell me shit when I'm high.

I should have listened.

I did listen.

Stop.

I think about the summer and it tastes like Doritos and warm beer that, in turn, tasted like failure. I got a sunburn that turned into a tan that peeled off in sheets, and Tanis and I did it again and again and again. And she said, "I love you." And I dove into the lake and my ears filled with water, and just for a few seconds I sank and couldn't remember how to swim, and then I swam.

The truth is that the only time I loved Tanis, really loved her, was when we were in that old fisherman's shack with the thick fog of cobwebs filling in all the sharp angles and the stink of old urine and dead mice. And we'd fucked up against the wall and she'd stared at me with her squinty eye and her regular eye. It was like diving into the lake.

I was always better at the dive than the swim. My swimming was always shitty, too much arm splashing and flailing, like a dog.

Tanis could swim pretty well, like a girl should. She dove into the water in her underwear, never naked. She'd put it back on before she swam, every time, coming up with her hair slicked back. Then she did look beautiful and like the models she wanted to be. But I never said and who cared? I smoked and smoked, in the water and out.

You can't smoke in the water.

Yes, you can. I did. A baggie tucked into my shorts, swimming to the raft and lying there, smoking, the sound of the water all around me and Tanis, and the whole time, of course, T-dot and Kate alone on the other side.

I thought they were eating chips.

I am a selfish dick and actually I didn't think about it at all. What they were doing. And it's none of my business.

Usually we took a Frisbee and a football and we played and the girls watched and the sun was hot and our skin burned and peeled more than once. And that's really all that happened this summer, except when it rained and we stayed home. Except when Gary was off duty and I was on.

Then it was different.

I hate T-dot because if Kate was skinny and hot, he would have told. And I hate him more because if I was fucking her, I wouldn't tell either. See?

Obviously.

But I thought *he* was a good guy. I guess I was wrong.

Anyway.

Summer. Last week. Last month. It was already a long time ago. I've already taken all my memories of it and edited them all together into one long scene, blurred by sunscreen on the lens and hidden behind a protective screen of smoke.

Yeah, like that.

I shoot the basketball. There is the nubby skin of it and there are my hands, my fingers finding the black grooves and the smell of the rubber is in my nose. It leaves my grip and soars into the sun, and I shield my eyes and watch it roll around the rim, once, twice, before falling, bouncing crookedly toward the girls, *slap slap* on the pavement.

"Hey," shouts the new guy, Phil Stars. "I was open."

"Sorry, man," I tell him. I'm not sorry. He's better than me, and I didn't throw it to him because he's better than me and I'm a jerk.

Tanis stands up. Throws it to me. I throw it to Stars. I am not a jerk, I'm just a guy. Just some kid. I pretend to not be me. I look at Tanis, cock my head. Sweat drips from my ear.

"I gotta get to work," she says. "Kiss me?"

And I am not me. I am playing the part of a guy with a girl who wants to be kissed. And I kiss her like people kiss on TV, bending her backward, my sweaty shirt making marks on her clean, white, dry clothes.

The first time I went to Tanis's house, I was pretty surprised. From outside, it looked like a normal crappy house. There used to be a mine just outside of town and there were a lot of mining houses left. Shitty little houses the company had built to house the employees. Hers was just another in a row all the same. But inside, inside it was different.

See on the ceiling, held up by wires, were these two cats. But they weren't regular cats. They looked like bobcats.

"What the hell are those?" I said.

"Oh," she said, looking up like she never noticed them. "Those are the cats that killed my mom."

The cats were posed like they were about to strike. Claws out. Their faces were stretched into messed-up snarls. I thought about her mom's DNA on those cat claws. Someone had to have cleaned that off.

"What?" I said, even though I heard her.

"My dad had them stuffed." She shrugged. "It made him feel better. It's symbolic, you know?"

"Oh," I said.

That is not true. That did not happen.

There are cats. Stuffed, dead cats.

They didn't kill her mom.

Her mom left.

I don't know the story of the cats.

Her dad is total whack job. He does security work at the bank and a couple of other places that no one would want to rob anyway. The only one worth robbing is the bank, but no one ever would. Tanis's dad is about six foot eight. He has a scar from his ear to the corner of his mouth. He shaves patterns into his beard that make him look like a pirate. He always looks like he's slept in his clothes, even when they're brand-new.

He's not, as they say, "all there."

After Dad jumped off the grain elevator, Tanis's dad painted it black, with skeletons all over it and a huge yellow bird at the top. He's some kind of fucked-up artist, I guess. You never know with people.

But I still don't understand how someone like Tanis came from someone like him.

Someone like Tanis.

There is no one like Tanis.

Sometimes she's explaining something to me about her ratios. How the whole world and everything in it can be understood in terms of beauty and explained once you understand the numbers. I want to believe her. I want to understand what she's saying. But mostly I just feel like a cartoon character, staring, mouth open, a huge question mark floating above my head.

Once I dreamed that her dad killed me and had me stuffed, but I was alive, and posed, claws out, over Tanis's bed. I woke up screaming.

Tanis says, "Whoa, you're getting me sweaty." But she doesn't really mind. I know she doesn't.

"Sorry," I say. But I'm not.

I wonder, does everyone lie?

I wonder, is there even a difference? Between lying and the truth?

I hold on to her and I can smell her hair, and it should be enough. Her hair smells different all the time. I don't know how she does that. Today it smells like strawberries. I am looking over her head for Olivia. Does she know Olivia? Are they in classes together? Do they sit close, sleeves touching?

"Hurry up, man," T-dot shouts. He's breathing heavily.

"Yeah, yeah," I say. "Just a second."

I hold on to Tanis tighter, and I don't know what I'm holding on to because she's pushing me away. Over her shoulder, I finally see Olivia slip out from under the shade of the oak tree that fills the whole parking lot with acorns and leaves. She climbs into a car that peels out of the parking lot on burnt rubber. I don't see who's driving.

And I shouldn't care, but I do.

chapter 9

I get home to find that Dad has fallen. Again. He sometimes forgets. He sometimes falls asleep and then when he goes to get up his legs don't work. That's what he says. He forgets. His head is bruised, a lump like an ostrich egg stretches purple and blue on his forehead.

"What the fuck?" I say.

"I fell," he says. "Don't make it a bigger deal than it is." His hand is shaking just enough to make him look old. He's holding on to a tiny pink bed. Tanis loves his dollhouses. He has the ratio right. The bed is made of wood. He's painted on the pink and even a few wrinkles in the sheet. I feel like the bed is growing in his hand. It's Chelsea's bed, of course. From when she was little. The bed is getting bigger and filling the room. I can't breathe. I look at Dad's head.

There's a rule about Chelsea: she cannot be mentioned. She doesn't see Dad. Ever. It's in the court documents. Never.

No contact.

I'm not allowed to know why.

I don't want to know why.

"It is a big deal," I say. "Where was Gary?"

Gary is a shitty care aide. I don't believe for a second that he even is one. He's a dealer, a biker, tattoos all the way up to his eyes. No kidding. Black and purple and blue and red and yellow and green. So much ink, you can't even tell what it is. He looks like a comic-book villain.

"Downstairs," Dad says. "Gary was downstairs. I've asked him to take over the processing. You're getting behind."

"What the fuck?" I say.

"I asked him to," he says. "It's a business and you're behind. He knows the business. It makes sense and you know it."

"It's *my* business," I say. "Fuck you, Dad. Fuck you. A thousand times, fuck you." I know I'm overreacting, but I can't help it. Dad looks like he's been clocked with a baseball bat in a cartoon. There is everything but a flock of birds, circling. Animated stars. It's hard to think clearly. He's not my kid, so why do I feel like he is?

I am not the father.

Dad sighs. "Nice language," he says. "What would your mother say?"

"She'd say, 'Fuck you,'" I say.

Gary wanders in. Gary *lumbers* in. His arms are pulling the fabric on the sleeves of his shirt so tightly that the shirt looks like a bandage. Gary looks at me slowly. Everything about Gary is slow. He's been smoking. His eyes are pink and dilated.

"What's up, kid?" he says.

"How's the basement?" I say sarcastically.

He shrugs. I hate him.

"Hey," says Dad. "Hey now. It's business. You're too busy and you have school." Glob takes a few steps toward me and nudges her head hard into my crotch. I pat her. She stinks like a wet wool sweater.

"Hey," says Dad again.

I glare at Gary and he glares back, and for a few seconds that's all there is. The shimmering heat waves of us glaring. Then something inside me collapses, and I just go, "Yeah. Whatever."

I stomp up to my room. The stairs that Dad can't climb make it so that the whole upstairs is mine. There are rooms I don't go in up here. I use only this one and the bathroom. If I go in the others, I'll have to clean them, and I can't be bothered. One of them is full of wet mold from a hole in the ceiling. At night, I'm pretty sure I hear things scampering.

My room isn't much better. I don't know who used to live in this room when Our Joe lived in this house. Someone who liked heavy metal. The old posters are curled around the edges. The tape has turned yellow. I leave them up because I figure it's kind of vintage cool. And I'm too lazy to take them down anyway.

Tanis says that Our Joe used to have foster kids. They got taken away.

She doesn't say why.

She does say why, but when she talks, her words come out garbled, like an old tape being eaten by the machine, and I try to hear her, but I can't, and I can't explain why I can't, so instead I just nod. I nod and nod.

Who loses *foster* kids? I hate Our Joe. I hate Gary. I hate my dad. I have so much hate I want to scream or vomit or tear the head off a chicken like the cartoon Ozzy is doing on the poster on my bedroom wall.

I can't stay in my room for long—it makes me antsy. Besides, Gary is here for a few more hours and I don't want to occupy the same space that he does. My muscles are twitching under my skin and I want to punch someone or something, so I switch into my running shoes and I go down the stairs again in one solid jump, landing so hard on the landing that the floor gives.

I don't want to think about floor rot. I am seventeen years old. I don't want to worry that our house is full of mice and, god knows, probably rats and the floors are rotting and the roof leaks and it's almost winter again and then what? It's cold.

I don't want to scream, "WHAT IS ALL THE MONEY FOR?"

We could buy a house. A real one. Somewhere else. I want to move to suburbia. Somewhere pretty, with green lawns and trees and kids playing hockey in the street.

Dad is back at the kitchen table. He slowly places a tiny couch in a tiny living room. He has to special order all this tiny furniture, but he paints it and decorates it. He sews these tiny cushions for the tiny chairs. He has really big hands. It's hard to see how that works, but it does. When he works, he sticks his tongue out slightly, like a kid learning to write.

Glob is at his feet. She is asleep, as she always is these days. Glob has cancer. Dad cannot have her put down because Glob saved his life, so Glob is as medicated as the rest of us, only she can't stay awake through it. Sometimes she snores. If you press on her belly, you can feel the lump.

Gary keeps giving me one of his slow looks. He is cooking something in the kitchen that smells like socks. He means something by the looks. I don't know what. I don't want everything to mean something. I know I am meant to know exactly what he is saying, but I don't *want* to know.

I just want to run.

I can *run*.

I step outside. The weather is ambivalent. I take a few steps and stop, and then start again. The gravel is slippery. I run down toward the corn. I have this weird feeling that I'll only be able to run so far and then the chain will snap and jerk me back, strangling me in the process. I rub my neck with my hand.

Nothing. I run faster.

I have weed in my pocket. Wrapped up tight. Processed by Gary. I stole extra this time. What the fuck kind of "processing" does weed need? You dry it, you bag it.

What else, Gary?

I run all the way back to the school, just to have someplace to go. I run hard, sprinting until I can't and jogging until the air comes back and sprinting again. Ugly, my feet hitting the edge of the road hard and avoiding broken glass and fast-food wrappers and a carton of milk tipped on its side in a white puddle, like someone threw it out the window of their car.

I get to the school and it's deserted. I'm too hot, my caged breath rasping out of me, full of spit and sweat. The sun is setting, and the sky is suddenly burning with the cold colors of orange sherbet.

I shiver.

I am looking for Olivia because if she isn't real then she is as likely to be here as not, right? If I am making her up, then I can make her be here.

Now.

But she isn't here. The air is still; it feels like there is about to be a thunderstorm. There is no one around but me. No one in the town, no one on the planet. I am so goddamn alone, and I wish I had a guitar and a microphone so I could sing something or scream it and someone would hear it. Somewhere.

The basketball court has dark shadows tipping over it, from the tree, the flagpole, the clouds starting to gather in the sky. The net hangs crookedly off the hoop.

My hands are empty. No guitar. No ball. I don't know what to do with them. I stare at them. Smack them together. Veins pulsing on the backs. My nails are dirty and too long. I sit on the cement steps and let the coldness of them seep through me until I've cooled off enough to shiver, my heart still pounding so hard in me that my eyes feel like they're vibrating. I watch cars pass and a lady with a dog, jogging. You don't see much of that here, so I watch her until she's gone.

Jiggle, jiggle.

And then I can breathe again.

I walk home. Slowly. Scuffing my shoes through the gravelly shoulder of the road that broadens to four lanes. The highway that cuts through the town. The trucks roar by and try to pull me into their slipstream.

Our Joe's farm is yellow in the sun. Green. It rolls around for miles. His ugly new house is up at the front, topping the gravel driveway like a bad, seriously-not-funny joke. A suburban palace, columns and glass. And he has no idea how ugly it is. He thinks people stare because it's amazing. Joe himself is on his front steps, and I'm relieved that he's dressed. He raises his hand in greeting and shouts, "TOUCHÉ!"

I have no idea what he means by that, but it pisses me off.

"Shut up," I shout back, and he laughs like I'm the funny kid I used to be. Did he know me then? I can't remember. I want so bad to hit him. I've never wanted to hit someone like I want to hit that old, pathetic, fucked-up, weird man.

Goddamn it.

My legs feel wobbly. I need to lie down.

I veer away, left, right. I stumble. I spin around. Then I'm there, in the corn.

Again.

Lost.

I like the way it feels, the randomness of a row. Like diving into the water from a different place each time and always ending up the same. T-dot once told me that diving into the water felt like coming home.

In the corn, I know what he means. I walk and walk. And maybe the part that is so familiar is the fact that I can't see my way, and a part of me is scared. The corn is high and thick. I turn in circles like a little kid, around and around and around, and way above my head a plane passes on its way to Vancouver. No one can see me. I spin until the corn tilts and then I fall, hitting my head on a stalk that doesn't give, the stalk leaving a claw mark on my cheek. I want it to puncture. I want it to go right through me. Threaded like a needle.

The dirt catches me. It's cool and damp. I lie still and the world tilts and swirls above me. The corn moves and bends. I light up and close my eyes and then open them again and pull all that sweet smoke deeper inside of me than anything ever goes.

And hold it.

If I could hold it forever, I would.

But eventually I have to exhale.

I wait.

And wait.

And wait.

And then.

chapter 10

EXT.—CORNFIELD—EARLY EVENING, SUNNY WITH CLOUDS GATHERING

And...

SCENE:

Dex Pratt is on his back in the cornfield.

He is alone.

No, scratch that. He is not alone. Maybe.

Dex Pratt is on his back in the cornfield. He is waiting. While he is waiting, he is smoking a joint from Gary's batch. Wheelchair weed, it's called. (Spot the irony.) It's strong. Somehow show that it's strong. Impossible. Never mind.

Show the wheelchair.

Show the plants.

Show that it's strong. How?

Dex is forgetting how to use the camera to show things.

Show Dex forgetting.

CUT TO:

INT.—X-RAY LAB

Show a picture of Dex's brain. Show how areas are being blurred out. Somehow connect that to this. Zoom in close to his whorls of gray matter and show that very close up they look like clouds. Show that very close up they look like smoke. Show that very close up they look like paths cut into the field of corn. Show that closer they are a map of the maze.

A kid in the middle. Tanis in the middle.

Crying.

She wants help. She is holding up a sign. The sign says, Help me, Dex Pratt.

Show Dex running away or running in place or squinting maybe like there is something too bright to look at in his path.

FLASHBACK TO:

INT.—LIVING ROOM

Show the stained couch. The way Dad hovers in the entryway, his wheelchair nearly too big for the space. The fireplace, filled with garbage that spills out onto the floor. Chinese food boxes on the coffee table. Empty. Disgusting.

DAD

I got good news, kid. You'll like these.

Show Dad throwing the bag of seeds at Dex. Dex startled, drops them. The bag of seeds looks like a…bag of seeds.

DEX

Whoopee.

DAD

This could make us rich, son. This is the stuff. You don't know what I had to do to get this.

DEX

Make some calls?

DAD

Yeah, something like that.

DEX

So, big whoop. I'll plant them, okay? I'll do it. Fine.

DAD

Yes, you will.

Show how Dad looked like he wanted to say more. Show how Dex picked up the remote, turned the volume up on a show just when the laugh track came on and for a minute the room was filled with laughter.

CUT BACK TO PRESENT:

DEX

This stuff tastes like shit.

Hold the camera above him and spin it.

Make the movie better. More artsy. This needs to be an artsy one. Consider the soundtrack carefully. Speed up the film and slow it down. Blur it and then make it so sharp that the edges glow.

Show the sky, filling slowly with dark clouds, black smudges of them, coal smears on the fake happiness of the blue. Because that's true. The clouds are gathering. People like weather in their movies. Weather sets the mood. Think of The Ice Storm. *Move the weather faster across the screen and then slower and then at hyperspeed.*

Show some wasps. Flying slowly.

Show the corn parting and someone is standing in front of Dex. The sun is shining in his eyes though. Still. Again. Show how he can't see who it is.

OLIVIA

I've been looking for you.

DEX

What?

OLIVIA

I'm here.

DEX

Who are you?

OLIVIA

I'm Olivia.

DEX

I know. I just can't think of the exact right thing to say to you that will make you understand what is happening here.

OLIVIA

Do you understand what is happening here?

DEX

No. I'm here.

OLIVIA

So am I.

Show Olivia sitting down next to Dex in the dirt. Show Dex having a fucking heart attack and dying.

DEX

This is stupid. I give up.

Show Dex giving up. Lying in the corn. Smoking. Eyes half shut. He is alone. Dex is always alone. His phone rings. Show Dex ignoring the phone. Show someone else standing in the corn. It's not Olivia; that's a stupid fantasy. It's Our Joe. He's watching Dex. Show Dex sitting up, becoming aware of someone staring.

DEX

What?

OUR JOE

That shit'll kill you, you know.

DEX

(lying back down)

Not hardly. It's natural.

Show how he is pretending to not be afraid. Show him taking off his shoes and using them to beat Our Joe to death. No, that's stupid. Cut that. Show him getting up and stretching. Show him thinking, pausing. Show him striking. No, cut that too. Show the truth: Show Dex doing nothing.

OUR JOE

Sometimes old people are wise.

DEX

True. Too bad you're not.

OUR JOE

Hey now.

DEX

What did you do, Our Joe? What did you do to her?

OUR JOE

(laughing)

She'll never tell.

Show Our Joe laughing. Make the laughter morph into a hyena's shriek. Show Our Joe turning into a hyena, slowly, grotesquely. Show him running away through the corn.

Show Dex turning into a lion and destroying him. Show Dex turning into a pussycat and falling asleep. Show Dex turning to stone. Show how he can't move.

Show Our Joe turning back into an old man wearing a red Speedo bathing suit and a turtleneck sweater with lurid yellow stripes. He appears to be carrying a fish. The flash of red and yellow in between the stalks of corn says that he's running. Can a man that old really run?

DEX

I just wanted one about Olivia, is that so wrong? Fuck you. I mean, fuck me. I mean... oh, forget it. Do I ever get what I want?

OLIVIA

Yes, you do, Dex.

But she isn't there. Was she ever there?

Take back the film. It's your film. It's your not-even-there-imaginary-camera and you are the director and the star, Dex Pratt. Take it back.

CUT TO:

INT.—A BEDROOM, ANY BEDROOM, MAYBE A HOTEL ROOM

Show how the room is messy. Show Dex, naked. Show Olivia, naked. Cut to the sex.

DEX

It's better if there is a story.

OLIVIA

There is always a story. Think about it. Didn't you make me up?

DEX

Yes. You aren't real.

OLIVIA

But I am. So maybe you're just psychic, maybe you predicted me.

DEX

Cut to the sex.

Play a lot of loud music. Make it look like a music video. It is a music video. Go back and edit out all the dialogue. The dialogue is the problem.

CUT TO:

EXT.—CORNFIELD

Show the weather changing. Black clouds clashing together like cymbals, rain falling, and lightning. (This part is real.) The soggy joint on the ground. Dex Pratt is sitting up, soaking wet, holding his head. Show Dex making his way through the corn. Show his false starts. Is it right or left? Which way did he come in?

Dex Pratt is lost in the cornfield. The corn is leaning under the weight of the sudden rain. Show the rain, falling so heavily that it becomes impossible to see anything else. A blur of rain. Play a song here. Maybe the one that was playing when Feral...

That one.

There is some kind of meaning in that. Show Dex's face. Show how there is no difference between raindrops and tears, and if you don't know which is which, what does it matter? Show him running. Lost. Show him screaming. Show that part again and again in slow motion.

Then show the dog. Show Glob, the ever-loyal golden, lumbering through the corn. Barking. Saving another Pratt.

Show Dex following the limping dog back home.

Then show Olivia. Show her. Soaking wet. Show her nipples in her see-through shirt. Show her face. Show her walking out of the corn, adjusting her jeans.

Imply something.

Imply everything.

Show Dex's phone. Still ringing. Tanis, it says on the screen in highlighted letters. Tanis Bowerman. Show Dex not answering, the phone ringing in the dirt, in the rain, where it will almost certainly be wrecked before he ever finds it again.

Things get lost that way.

chapter 11
september 14, this year.

It is the second week of school, and for seven days I haven't seen her. The Girl. *Olivia.* I like that name. I hate that name. I made up that name, so I can change it. Now she's Madison. No, she's not.

Olivia.

Anyway, she's gone.

I am starting to relax and then...

There.

She is.

Olivia is wearing a motorcycle jacket over a white dress. She is wearing rubber boots. Her hair shines. It moves in slow motion when she walks. Smooth today, not surfer chic. It's longer. That's impossible, but it is. Her dress is translucent enough to kill me.

Do you care about the weather? Really?

Okay.

It's windy, but the sky is mostly clear. White clouds strung out like something sticky stuck to the universe's shoe. The air smells like leaves that are just starting to turn, a damp, cold cloth and the chemical waft of pesticide.

I am running up the cement steps, two at a time. I am not in the mood to deal with Stacey or Mr. V today. Again. (Three times last week was too many.) I am trying to remember without looking whether English! is up first, or maybe Careers!

But Olivia wants to be thought about.

She sits on the steps, straight-backed, toes pointed in. Her skirt is hitched up high enough that I can see a dusting of fine, blond hairs on her knees. The crowd of kids parts around her like the Red Sea. No one talks to her.

Why doesn't anyone talk to her?

She is waiting for me. But the thing is, I can't think of a thing to say. Something about the weather. Or Math! No, that's not good enough.

Nothing that I think of is good enough. My brain is made of grinding metal gears, a dusting of rust falling around my feet. "I...," I start. She doesn't hear me. My voice is a frog's croak. A really tiny frog. The kind you only notice when you step on it with bare feet.

There are thirteen stairs between me and her, and I don't know if she has seen me yet. People pass between us in a group, younger kids, jostling. One of them falls and pushes hard against me, and I push him back up again. For a second he hangs in the air, and then he's gone.

Kate says, "Move it, Pratt." She is suddenly behind and beside me. She stares at my face. "Hey," she says. "Seriously, move." She looks disgusted. She glances at Olivia but doesn't say anything. "Tanis says to meet her at her locker, 'kay?"

"Sure," I say. My hand is still in midair, about to greet Olivia. Kate walks right through her.

I lower my arm and blink. Once. Twice. My heart does a scuttle in my chest like a cockroach on a hardwood floor.

Olivia's eyes settle on me, then away, then back. She pushes her glasses up her nose. I can't move. I want her to move. Get up. Say something. She is so still. She's made of salt. She's dissolving. She's there. My heart speeds up and I think about how I was...you know, in the cornfield. About how I was jerking off and thinking about Olivia, pretending. And I'm sure she knows, the way she's smiling. She knows and I'm going to die and then come back to life and then die again. The blush starts somewhere below my abdomen and works its way up, and I start marching up the stairs again, right past her. I don't stop. I look over her head like I don't even see her.

I glance back at her, once I'm past, and I think she shakes her head, just a bit, like a dog shaking an irritating fly out of her ear, or a bird flapping free of a wire.

I want her to be normal.

I want me to be normal.

I want a joint.

I need one. I feel in my pocket. Need, want. Want, need. Maybe I have time. Behind me, two girls are talking about a concert in the city they are going to.

"Rad," one says.

"Fucking rad," the other agrees. "I've got the car."

"Awesomely fucking rad," the other one says. "Do you have my red shoes?"

"No," says the other one. "You never let me wear your stuff, remember?"

"TANIS!" I yell.

It's not like Tanis is out here, so I don't know why I do that.

"Tanis," I mutter.

I hurry to Tanis's locker and I spin her and dip her and she laughs and I make myself smile. People stare. They look at us and think we're in love or something equally bullshitty. They are jealous, but they don't know what is real and what is just pretend. Tanis is my fake girlfriend. I'm fake and she is not. I almost drop her and then hoist her back up. She cocks her head and says, "Wanna come over after school? I didn't get a shift today."

And I say, "Absolutely." Even though I know I can't and I don't want to and everything I say is a lie. I have practice.

Sometimes I just want to say, "Yes," to Tanis. Yes and yes and yes and yes and yes. I want her to explain me. I want her to tear me apart and put me back together, ratios in place. Instead I cough. I pretend to cough. I pretend like I didn't just about burst into tears. I cough and cough. She pats me on the back, "Whoa," she says. "Don't die."

I shake my head. "I won't," I say. "I won't."

Every time I see Olivia in the hallway, I pretend I don't. I edit her out of my film. Where she is standing, I edit in puce-colored lockers. A zitty-faced kid. An overflowing garbage can.

I try to talk to Tanis about normal stuff. I go, "Who'd you have for English?" and "Why're you taking Metal Shop?" I say, "You've got to listen to this song," and I jam my iPhone earbud into her ear so she can hear too. I touch her leg. Everything I say feels stilted and untrue. I say, "My dad hit his head again." I say, "I fucking hate math."

When Tanis looks at me, I can feel her calculating and making me okay. She's mentally measuring the distance between my nose and my lip. The proportion of my ears.

She draws a sketch of me on a blank piece of paper and presses her lips on it and gives it to me. It has a wrinkled lip print that looks repulsive. It's not her but the print that skeeves me out. I shudder and she takes it back, balls it up and texts Kate.

Tanis is always texting Kate. I want her to talk to me like she talks to Kate, but Kate has a million things to say and all I can say is, "Crows freak me out." Just as one swoops down and grabs an entire lunch bag from the garbage can.

Tanis eats lunch sitting on my lap, and she traces my cheeks with her fingertips. I try to stop my mind from spinning. I try to concentrate on something, anything. I try to not look over her shoulder for Olivia, but I am, because I can't not. Then I go to Math! Bio! Careers!

I get through the day, and Olivia is everywhere, just watching. She is smiling but also isn't. Her dress is see-through when she passes windows. Still. Again. She isn't there.

She is.

She's wearing a white dress. But when I see her again, it's the same dress and it's blue.

I pass her closely and I smell vinegar and spice.

I don't know what she wants from me. What could she want from me?

Nothing.

Everything.

Besides which, I don't for a second believe she's real.

Our school is serious about very little, but basketball matters. Probably because Mr. V used to be some kind of college star. If Mr. V is the future of being a college star, I don't want to be one.

Practice is good. The new guy is killer. Phil Stars. He's better than me. Way better. But I already knew that.

Today I like him because he is better than me. I like that he is better than me. No one would believe me, but it's true.

"He's just having a good day," whispers Tanis.

"Nah," I tell her. "He's better. It's okay."

"No way," she says. She doesn't get it. She says, "It's just straight-up because he's taller and has longer arms, Dex."

"Doesn't matter," I say. I want him to be better. It takes some of the pressure off me to be good. There is a lot of pressure.

Even my dad, this morning, while I made his eggs, said, "Practice starting today, huh?"

"Yep," I said. "I guess."

"You know, son," he said—and I knew what he was going to say was going to be a Dad thing because "son" is reserved for Dad *things*. "Son," he said, "basketball might just be the thing that changes your life."

I shrugged it off. "I'm not that good," I said. I was annoyed. Everyone thought I was this superstar, but they were wrong. I was good, but not good *enough* to matter. But Dad needed me to be this super athlete. Maybe it was as simple as I was supposed to use my legs because he couldn't use his. Besides, my life had already changed quite enough. Once. Twice. Enough times that I couldn't keep up. The last thing I wanted was more fucking *change*.

"You are that good," he said. "You could get scholarships."

"I don't need scholarships, Dad," I said. I was getting mad. The eggs were burning. Sweat was dripping off my lip, but it wasn't hot in the room. It was just anger. The low simmer.

"Why not, son?" he said. He rolled closer. I smelled piss. He does his own catheter and he obviously messed up. I hesitate. Should I say something or pretend I don't notice?

"I'm sleeping on thousands of goddamn dollars, Dad," I said through gritted teeth. "Probably could pay my own way to school."

"Oh?" he said. "You could, could you? Is it *your* money now?"

"It's *my* pot," I mumbled.

"If I wasn't in this chair, I'd kick your ass for that," he said. "I would." He stared at me. "What is going on in your head?"

If only he knew what a good question that was.

I almost answered him. Almost.

"Dad," I said, "don't try to get all Dad-like on me now. It's too late for that." I turned off the eggs but I didn't put them on his plate. I just left them there in the fry pan, too high for him to reach.

In the hot pan, they probably did burn. Gary could cook him some new ones. Gary could take care of it. Gary, Gary, Gary.

Fuck Gary.

Maybe Gary wanted to be his fucking son. Gary could have the job. I sure didn't want it.

I was halfway to school before I started to hate myself for that little stunt. Before I started to want to go back, give Dad his eggs and say sorry. But sorry for what, that's what I didn't really know.

Which is why I walked so slowly. Because of the weight of that.

Which is why I was late.

Which is why I never saw Olivia that morning on the steps and why Kate did not walk through her. Why I know my brain is looping around in a way that isn't right and the ratio of sane to crazy has tipped the wrong way, and no amount of smart math can undo that.

I am playing basketball, and practice is over but I don't want to stop playing. I gulp down bottle after bottle of

Gatorade and picture myself sweating blue, like in the commercials. I drink more and more.

Coach claps his hands. "Nuff," he says. "Change room, showers, move it."

The team moves. Lots of clapping each other on the back. Lots of sweat. Lots of dripping.

Then no one is left but me and T-dot.

"One time?" I say.

"One time," he says. He crouches low. I grab the ball.

Coach is in his office. He looks up every once in a while and points to the change room. He's choosing the captain. It's not going to be me. I'm happy.

The ball keeps flying through the hoop, leaving my hands like it's charmed, the hollow sound of it bouncing onto the wood floors, again and again, the bang of it against the backboard, our harsh breathing. The sweat is spattering everywhere. And there is the stink of it and the sound of our sneakers on the floor of the gym, which makes me feel like I'm ten or eight or twelve or some other age than seventeen, some age from *before*. The squeak is what I think of first when I think of being a kid in school. When I think of first grade.

Sneaker squeak at assemblies, games, gym class. The dusty smell of the gym. The layers of sweat that line the floor.

The skin of the basketball is more familiar to me than anything, anyone, ever. I want to absorb it. Somehow.

I want to hold the ball so tight that I become it and it becomes me. The sweat is dripping from my nose like a fucking nosebleed, salty and unstoppable. And I am holding the ball so tight it might explode in my hands, shards of rubber everywhere. And there is something else, while I'm there in the gym with T-dot, my best friend. There is the knowledge that *I'm better, I'm better, I'm better than him.* It is in my blood and in my sweat and everywhere, like something Alice drank when she fell down the well. I am not better than Phil Stars, but I am better than T-dot. And so what and so what and so what? Why do I even care?

I loosen my grip on the ball and spin it and bounce it, and *bam*, it's back in my hands, like it belongs there, like it's alive and it's choosing.

Choosing *me*.

I throw the ball hard to T and it whoomps into his chest. He winces in pain and says, "Settle down."

I go, "One more set."

He goes, "I don't know, man. I gotta get home."

"One more," I say. "Or are you scared I'll beat you again?"

He shrugs.

T-dot's got a scholarship to a university Down Under in Melbourne, Australia. He's a fucking good swimmer. The kind of good that gets money and medals. The kind of good that I am not. Not at basketball. Not at anything.

"Over here, mate." "Bad call, mate." "Hit the rim, mate." "Mate, mate, mate," I say, like it's funny. And he is grinning. When he does that, I can remember us being nine and twelve and fourteen and how we laughed. And it makes me madder. Mate, mate, mate. Throw a shrimp on the barbie, mate. His jaw is popping and he keeps saying, "Hey." Like as in, "Hey, let up." Or, "Hey, SHUT UP."

I remember how me and T-dot built this skateboard ramp once. I don't know why I'm suddenly thinking of it, but I am. I almost go, "Hey, remember the ramp?" but then he scores and swaggers around the court, high-fiving the air, and then I'm pissed again. The ramp was a long time ago. Before Vancouver.

Before Mom met her man.

Before Feral discovered smack.

Before Dad jumped.

Before I went from someone who thought that "fun" happened after a Slurpee and half-pipe to someone who thought he could control the party to someone who only knew how to fake it.

The ramp went halfway up a tree and then curved down and around, and it was amazing. Even now, I don't know how we built that. It was good. Back then, all we could talk about was skating and how great it would be when we grew up and we'd never stop. Did you ever notice how you rarely see an adult on a board? And that wasn't going to be us.

We thought that was hilarious.

Everything was *awesome* and *dude* and nothing mattered, not really, and we'd fight about which band was better or which cola. And we'd laugh most of the time, almost all the time, like we were young, which we were. All that fucking laughing. Like maybe we laughed so much, we used up our quota. Or I did.

Not T-dot. He's still laughing.

But now I am a thousand years old and he's still young. That's the thing that isn't *fair*.

"Awesome, dude," I say. But it doesn't sound the way it used to sound when I said it. It sounds different.

He shoots me a look. "Yeah," he says. "Look, I gotta go."

"One more," I say.

That's what I say.

I grab the ball and I hold it up so he can't reach.

"Jump, kangaroo, jump," I say. It comes out mean. His eyes are pissed but he is laughing because that's T-dot, and he reaches up for the ball and I jump to hook the shot over his head, a show-off shot, you know, and I fall.

As I hit the ground, there is a pop from the inside of my knee that right away makes me think of grapes. A grape on the floor that you carelessly step on and it pops. And then splayed flat there on the floor, it no longer looks anything like a grape.

My knee immediately no longer looks like a knee. I don't know how long I sit there for. A few seconds or forever.

"Holy shit," says T-dot. "Oh man. Dex." He gets right down on his knees and holds my knee in his hands.

"Fuck off," I say. "Don't touch me, you perv."

Like he is *touching* me.

He pulls his hands back like I've burned him, which I have. I can see the look on his face. The gym floor is slippery underneath me. Wet with our sweat. I smell dust. The painted lines are worn and blurry. Or maybe my eyes are blurry.

I am not goddamn *crying*.

T-dot disappears and comes back with ice and the coach. Coach is a small wiry guy. He jumps around nervously and says "ACL" six or seven times. I close my eyes and there are white dots there, bright white lights of pain and I can't get my breath all the way in or out.

"I just want to go home," I say.

"You gotta go to the hospital, kid," he says. "We gotta get you an MRI."

"It will still be messed up tomorrow," I say. "I'll do it tomorrow, okay?"

T-dot goes, "I'll take him home."

"You can't go home!" says Coach. "You gotta get it looked at."

He has a tuft of black hair sticking out of his nose. His hands are nervous. They are scratching his bald head like talons. White flakes drift down. What does it matter? I think. It's already over. No one's knee does this and then gets better. He can write me off. But he's got the new guy, the tall guy. He'll be fine. I want to say this, but instead I just go, "I'm fucking going home, okay?"

T-dot is quiet. He stands under my arm like a crutch, and we hobble to the parking lot. He doesn't say anything. I don't say anything.

The van stinks of chlorine.

By the time I get home, the nausea is all up in me. Car sickness. From the smell, I think. I stand in the driveway and wait for him to leave, and I don't say thank you or goodbye or anything, and he just lifts his hand in farewell. When he's gone, out of sight, I puke in the shrubbery. I sit down on the ramp that Dad uses to go in and out of the house. I stare into the corn and I think: I am a prick and I deserve this.

I do.

Don't for a second think that I don't.

chapter 12
september 16, this year.

I am self-medicating.

It's *natural*.

I am lying down in the cornfield.

My hair is full of dirt. When I sit up, it's going to fall down all over me like clumps of black hail, like my own private storm. I can feel the soil, cool on the back of my neck like a million tiny zombie fingers touching me.

On my way to lunch today, Olivia stopped me in the hall. She leaned forward and whispered in my ear. I didn't hear what she said, and you can't ask someone to repeat a whisper. It's too intimate. And I didn't want her to touch me because any touch threw me enough off balance that my knee screamed in agony in a way that I could only pretend to ignore.

The ground is damp and the corn is high and so am I. The "I" in that sentence stretches like a bungee cord. Iiiiiiiiiiiii.

Hiiiiiiiiigh.

I laugh. Laughing when you are alone is...

My laugh is like small brown birds hopping on my face and chest. Pecking.

I stop laughing and the silence is water.

I am smoking four or five times a day now. I must stink. I don't care that I stink.

I cannot feel my knee.

It's seeeerious. My brain stretching out like taffy. I've never seen taffy. What the fuck is taffy?

My brain stretches for miles. The last sweet corn of the season stretches for miles, waiting. It goes on forever, into the horizon. It *is* the horizon.

The corn is making waves with the wind. The corn is the sea. If the corn were the sea, I'd already be drowned, lungs full, heart slowing. And the sun would be wavering above something green and glassy and impenetrable. Just like that.

Over and out.

It's corn, not water. I'm not dead. I'm breathing; look at me. In and out. Out and in. Too fast, too slow, too raspy, too dry. I need a drink so bad. Water. I'd die for water, but I don't move. Because I can't.

I hold my breath as long as I can, and my eyes hurt and my ears. And then I let it out and tears are streaming down my cheeks and getting lost in my hair, in the dirt, in the seaweed.

There's no *seaweed.*

I never swam in the sea even when I lived in Vancouver and the sea was everywhere. The sea is too cold, too dirty, too full of teeth.

T-dot can swim underwater for so long that you think he's drowned, but you know he hasn't because you can see him moving, a big dark blur like a shark lurking below you.

I haven't gone swimming with T-dot for years. Haven't seen him swim. I don't even know him anymore. T-dot is just another prop in my act. He is my "friend." Tanis is my "girlfriend."

I am acing this project. The project of faking "me."

Maybe I could get a special-project grade at school. Some kids who live on farms get random A's for "special projects" like cross-breeding cows or inventing an egg.

I pull deeply on the joint, and my lungs are blanketed by the gravy-thick unbreathability of it. It's like smoking an animal, something once alive and now dead.

The corn moves like girls, swaying low. Humming.

I am humming.

The ground is humming. Somewhere under me there are a million bugs so tiny you need a microscope to see them. I wish I had one, but I'm also glad I don't. If you have a microscope, you're probably obligated to keep finding tiny things and inspecting them. Problem is, I'd never know what I was looking for.

I have all these thoughts. They are shiny on the edges, like a migraine or a potato wrapped in foil. I am thinking in words.

I am thinking this:

I. Am. So. Baked. Over and over again, like a mantra. If my mom could see me now, would she care?

Check one:

A) No.

B) Not really.

C) I doubt it.

"I am so baked," I say out loud, and my voice is crumbly and dry like balled-up paper, so I stop talking, because that's just psycho to lie in a cornfield talking to yourself. Next stop, Crazy. Straitjackets provided, free of charge.

I lie in the cornfield and there is no mental movie. Not this time. The shit is strong enough that the movie doesn't even start, and I am free.

Just me and the pot and the stretched-out air.

chapter 13
september 20, this year.

There are things I'm leaving out.

Important things.

I don't know why I'm leaving them out. Lately, I've been confused. It's hard to know where to edit your own life. Which parts to leave. Which parts to erase. Movies top out at two hours before the audience starts tuning out. True fact.

I will tell you some things I've cut:

Feral is not dead.

Tanis and I fucked on the night we met. Re-met. In the car. Afterward, I felt like I'd been turned inside out. It wasn't Tanis's fault. She said, "I don't do that." She cried. And she probably doesn't. As a rule anyway.

I changed her. I told her it was okay, that I didn't think less of her, but secretly I was happy that she was a slut, because then I could feel that she wasn't quite good enough for me.

Mom calls me every night and I refuse to take the call. Dad talks to her. For about an hour after he's done on the phone, he's smiling.

The smile kills me.

I talk to Chelsea on Sunday nights at ten, which is past her bedtime. Chelsea is my sister. I'm leaving her out on purpose.

Those are some of the things I left out.

I think that there are more.

chapter 14
september 21, this year.

Dad is in bed. His room smells like mold and mothballs and BO and piss and worse. I need to do his laundry. His sheets are my job, not Gary's. Gary has all my old jobs. He showers Dad and changes him. He does the pot. He does everything. Dad's sheets are crusty. I try not to think about it.

I think he's waiting for me to notice.

I half limp, half slide into the house. I want to tell him about this, whatever it is, that I have smoked and how it's messed me up, but my tongue is both too big and too small to form words. My knee looks like a zombie's brain.

I stand in the doorway of Dad's room and watch him pretending to sleep. I can always tell when other people are faking. Underneath the other stinks, his room smells like a hospital room. I don't know why. There isn't any reason. I never clean it, so you can't blame Pine-Sol. Glob is lying next to Dad. She will lie next to him forever.

Sometimes when Dad thinks I'm not home, I hear him talking to Glob in the way that I wish he'd talk to me. He talks about things that are interesting. Shit he heard on the news. A book he read. Just things. The weather. The way his mom used to fry chicken.

Dad never talks to me about just *things*.

He opens his eyes and looks at me. "Son," he says, "go to bed."

"My knee's worse," I say, which isn't true, but it isn't a lie either. I don't know what I want from him.

Dad sighs, like he's asleep, which I know he isn't.

"We'll talk about it tomorrow," he says. He holds so still that I almost think he's holding his breath. I flick off his light switch and leave him to it. Limp up the stairs. The pain in my knee is unbelievable, like by just saying that it's worse, it got a lot worse.

Every step, it feels like something is tearing.

I flop down on my bed and call Tanis.

She answers, out of breath. She's on her bike, riding home from work.

"It's okay," she says. "Hang on. I'll just stop, so we can talk."

"Come over," I say.

"I can't," she says. "I'm doing a project."

Tanis does projects. The one she is working on is the town, done entirely to scale. She is making a map of her life. All over town, there she is, in miniature, at different ages. The farms are carefully demarcated. The whole thing takes up their entire rec-room floor. Her dad is cool about it. In the parking lot of Safeway, she's put my dad's car. Dad would like this shit. He would understand the need to make things tiny. It's only me that's left out of the joke.

Is it a joke?

I don't know.

She says she got the idea from him. It fits her perfectly though because it involves her math and his art. I feel like they are ganging up on me, and it makes no sense because they barely talk.

"Please come over, Tanis," I say. "I need you."

She hesitates. I can picture her biting her lip, and I get a hard-on just imagining her face. I know she'll come.

"Okay," she says. "Just for a while."

"Long enough," I say. I grin. I throw the phone into the laundry basket with a bunch of fetid laundry. I am always throwing my phone and it is always somehow coming back to me. I lie back and wait for Tanis to come and take care of me.

Don't I deserve at least that?

My knee hurts so fucking much.

I've never had anything hurt this bad. Not ever.

chapter 15
september 21, this year.

Here is another one of the things that I left out:

When I came home from school on the first day, Gary was punching my dad in the head. I saw it through the screen. My dad's head snapped backward and then lolled forward like a bobblehead in a car crash.

Gary looked up and saw me.

My dad did not.

I waited on the front steps for twenty-five minutes. I smoked a joint and listened to four songs on my iPod. Then I swung open the door and went in.

"What happened to your head?" I shouted at my dad. I wasn't mad at him until I saw him, just sitting there like nothing had happened.

chapter 16
september 22, this year.

Tanis drives me to school in my dad's car. I've been driving, but every time I have to punch the clutch, I scream in pain. This is better.

Tanis stayed the night and my dad is furious. He has lines, he says. And I've crossed them.

I make a mental list of my dad's "lines":

Doing drugs? Okay.

Having sex? Not okay.

I am grown-up enough to be the man of the family and I am also not. I am the kid. Have I forgotten that I'm the kid?

Yes, Dad. I *have*.

When we got up this morning, sweaty and sleepy, the alarm scaring the crap out of me, Dad was waiting for us in the kitchen. In his chair, he looked regal, like a man on a throne. If you overlooked the fact that he was in his pajamas and smelled like he hadn't showered in days, that is. He had three days of stubble. His beard was gray now. It made him look old.

He didn't look at either of us while he spoke, but he said all the things that proper dads are supposed to say. I was nearly proud of him. Right up until the part where he called Tanis a slut and me a loser.

He might be right about me, but he should have left Tanis out of it.

She holds the steering wheel so tightly, her knuckles are white. She is mad at *me*.

"You don't fucking understand anything, Dex," she says. The windows are steamed up. I want to roll the window down but that might be rude, so I don't.

"I do understand," I say. "I'm sorry. It was my fault and my dad is a total wang. What do you want me to say?"

"I don't know," she says. When she's mad, the bad side of her face gets even more scrunched up than normal. She looks bad. Her hair is flat on one side where she fell asleep on my chest. I should probably find that sexier than I do.

"I'm sorry," I say again. "You aren't a slut."

"That's not why I'm mad!" she says. "God, you're so freaking stupid. Don't you get it? I'm wearing the same clothes as yesterday. Everyone's going to know." Then she says, "You're making me someone I'm not, you fucking idiot."

"My knee hurts," I say. The whole time she's yelling at me, my knee has been pulsing with this pain that feels like something gnawing at my flesh from the inside. The pain has taken over my whole body. It's radiating everywhere like some kind of internal octopus of pain, arms stretched to cover all of my flesh. "I'm not making you anything. You are who you are."

"Fuck you," she mutters.

I think I probably should go to the hospital. I probably need some kind of surgery.

But I can't have surgery.

Who would take care of Dad? *Gary*?

Forget it.

"You're not even listening!" she yells. Then she bursts into tears. I don't know how to deal with tears.

"I'm sorry," I say again.

Her lips are moving. Numbers, numbers. She whispers 25:15 and 16:209. Her knuckles are so white, it hurts to look at them.

We pull into the parking lot and I see Olivia getting out of a car. This time I get a good look at the driver. An older man, probably her dad. I'm relieved.

Tanis looks at me looking at Olivia. "No fucking way," she says.

"What?" I say. Then I go, "Do you see her?"

"I can't believe you, Dex Pratt," she says. "You are too much."

I don't know if that means that she sees Olivia or not. "Is she real?" I say, before I can stop myself. Tanis gets out of the car, leaving the keys in. We aren't even in a parking stall. She storms off. When she's mad, she walks like she's on a catwalk. I half expect her to turn and spin.

I think about proportions. I try to think about proportions. I think about why proportions matter so much to Tanis.

I think about how no one knows about Tanis's proportions but me.

I think about the proportion of time passing to time needed.

Needed to do what? There is nothing I need to do. I put a pencil through the stretcher in my ear. When I first ran into Tanis, she leaned across the counter of Safeway and said, "Whenever I see someone with one of those things in their ears, I want to put a pencil in it."

I think about leaving a pencil in it all day to make her laugh.

I have to park this car now. People are honking and going around me and staring. They think I'm crazy because of the way I'm acting. Because of the way I'm overacting. They can tell that I am not being me.

Or, more likely, they don't care and I'm in the way.

I struggle to lift myself over the stick shift and slide into the driver's seat. The pencil pokes my cheek awkwardly. My earlobe is twisting. I take the pencil out.

I drive the car into the last parking spot and now I am late. I have to limp all the way up the stairs and that just seems like too much. So instead, I just sit in the car.

I sit and I sit. I sit in the car for the entire day of school until my bladder feels like it's gonna burst, and then I drive home. I don't know how many people see me there, sitting in the car. But no one comes over. Not one person comes to see if I'm okay.

chapter 17
september 23, this year.

I am in the corn again. I saw a horror movie about corn once. I saw a documentary about corn once.

Corn is the cheapest food in the world.

Cornfields house psychopathic kids wielding weapons.

Corn is almost all genetically modified.

Even this corn is probably not what it appears to be: strong, green, healthy.

It's the last corn of the season. It's so sweet now, it's like biting into candy. Even raw.

The rats are on a sugar high.

In Vancouver, we had this tree in the yard with dark red leaves, and if you lay under it and looked straight through it at the sun, you could see a silver outline around each and every leaf. But pull the leaves off and bring them in to inspect, and they were just red leaves, dark and flat.

It was a trick. The light can do that.

I feel like I could write, but I haven't written a single word since I left Vancouver. I used to write lyrics. For our band. Mine. And Feral's.

I wrote good lyrics.

When Mom married Feral's dad, we became brothers. We used to talk so much. I feel like I've forgotten how to talk. I never talk about anything anymore. I try to listen to other people talking, and it seems like they don't know how either.

Ninety percent of conversations are about nothing.

I could write good lyrics about that. Or about just *this*. The corn and the cobweb that's hanging above me and the slanting sunlight and those aluminum-rimmed words. But as soon as I think of what, exactly, I'd write, as soon as I try to squish all these microscopic yellow/blue/brown/green metallic thoughts into some kind of black and white sentence, it's gone, like a dream dripping out of my head even as I'm still watching the end of it play out.

Anyway, fuck that.

I sit up.

I lie down.

My ab muscles pull taut and loose. I lift my shirt and look at them. I have good abs. Maybe I could be a model.

No matter how I look at the future, it all seems unlikely and ridiculous. Is there a future?

I was kidding about the modeling. There's the laugh again. The brown birds of it on my chest.

My summer-brown skin is speckled with sprinkler dew. How did I get so brown? I was at the lake a lot. I hardly ever wore a shirt. When I was at home, I sat outside and read books and pretended to not hear my dad calling me. I found a box of books in the basement.

I read *Moby Dick*.

It's true.

I read books of poetry about red wheelbarrows and felt like I understood but maybe that's because I was high. I started getting high in the spring. I never sampled the crop before. But when I started, I couldn't stop.

Won't stop.

Can't stop.

Maybe that's what it was like with Feral and the heroin. *Obviously* that's what it was like with Feral and the heroin. I'm not an idiot. I know what addiction is. I don't know why the heroin didn't catch me like it did him. Maybe I wasn't worth bothering. When I picture heroin, it's a pale-skinned man, dark hair slicked back, a wolfish grin, tight suit, hands with long nails painted like a girl's, promises he can't keep. He toyed with me and took Feral, laughing the whole time.

Fuck him. Fuck him. A million times fuck him. He didn't want me. I could care less about heroin. But the lumpy, old, stinky, aging surfer who is pot has me in his grip and he won't let me off the board. Ever. We'll drown together.

There are crows in the cornfield. They peck back the husks and fill their bellies with the sugar-sweet corn. They call each other, and more and more and more come until the blackness of their feathers is the norm and the crows are only noticeable in places where they aren't.

I could write that.

Do people still write poems? What a bullshitty thing to do. Imagine saying it out loud, "Oh, I wrote a *poem*." Worse than "I'm a model," but not by much.

I'd punch me for that. A solid punch. Fist to bone. Red blood. The surprise factor of the pain. Someone shouting.

But still, a goddamn poem. Take *that*.

I close my eyes and try thinking only about *words* to block out the movies that want to come that I don't want to see. There is one movie, lying in wait for me.

Starring my dad.

And my mom.

I am not going to let it start. The mist is coming off the sprinklers, making small rainbows between me and that blue sky, which is starting to sink down on my chest like a giant knee, pinning me. There are flies, dark clouds of them, shifting the air around. A giant knee. Why did I say *knee*?

I don't want to think about knees, not that I can stop thinking about my knee because of the pain of it and because I know it means that there will be a shift. I won't be an athlete anymore, so I'm going to have to find a different role to play. I've exhausted all the ones I can think of.

Maybe now I should be the bad guy. Take this drug thing and run with it. Expand.

Why not?

I've already been everything else.

The brain, the jock, the musician, the filmmaker, the athlete, the nurse, the horticulturalist.

I roll over, facedown in the dirt. I can feel it in my nose. Chemicals, rocks, bugs, dirt. I think about earthworms, their long elastic bodies stretching taut, their blind eyes reaching for the darkness. My heart is galloping away from me. Seriously, that's how my mind says it: "My heart is galloping away from me." When I thought that, I could see it, a black horse. A black horse trying to breathe but snorting instead. Foaming at the mouth.

There are fewer horses in this town than you'd think. Being a farm town and all. People always imagine horses. Glass gave me a cowboy hat when I moved back here.

It's brown. I told her it wasn't small-town like on TV. I told her there were no horses.

I think Zach Meyer's ranch is the only one in town, and even then it's outside of town. So it really doesn't count.

I can hardly remember Glass. We dated for almost two years and I can't really remember anything specific except that she panted when we kissed, like she was only occasionally remembering to come up for air.

I can't breathe.

I should roll over, but I don't.

The dirt is filling up my mouth, and then I come up, suddenly choking on it, like I just remembered I couldn't swim.

Only I, Dexter Pratt, could be enough of an asshole to actually drown myself in a fucking *cornfield.*

I am going to break up with Tanis. It isn't her fault. It's Olivia's.

"It's over," I say in my papery voice. And the words are all scrunched up in my mouth, and so I spit and spit and spit, and it has a tang like tin and not like soil at all.

Tangs are fish. Those bright ones you see in dentist's offices. When did all dentists decide that fish were *de rigueur*?

I'm soaked cold from the sprinklers.

I stand up and my knee screams from the pain of it, and for a second I think I might black out. I force myself to stand tall. Just me, taller than the corn, my filthy head sticking up above the surface like a zombie slowly rising from the depths, all wide red eyes and stealth. I wait and there's nothing but the machine-gun sound of the sprinklers and a bird flying between me and the clouds, making them seem somehow extra3-D. I scratch my hair greedily, like I can't get enough. Then I head for home, my phone buzzing in my pocket, bloodsucking mosquito buzzing in my ear.

Nothing ever happens in the corn. Not really.

No ax-murdering toddlers.

No blood.

That's why I like it.

It's everything that happens when I'm not in the corn that's the problem.

chapter 18

INT.—DEX'S BEDROOM

Show that Dex is asleep in bed. Show his room. Show all the filthy dishes. Show his pile of unopened homework books. Show the stains on the sheets. Show how when he sleeps, his arms are thrown back above his head so that every morning when he wakes up, his arms feel unattached. Zoom in on his knee.

Show Dex half waking.

DEX

Not now. Stop it before it starts, Dex.

DEX

Fuck this.

Show Dex getting up and opening his laptop. Show Dex clicking on a small icon. Show the movie starting. It's an old home movie that someone has uploaded and dumped into the computer. The film is jittery, like old home-movie films are. The VHS *tape had obviously started to degrade.*

Show Dex watching the movie.

The camera is being held at ground level. Whoever is holding it is under a bed. It is Dex's parents' bed. Let the viewer listen to the sound of kid breathing.

Show the shadows and dust under the bed.

DAD

You bitch. I can't believe you did that.

MOM

I didn't do it!

DAD

I don't believe you. And I have proof.

MOM

You had me followed? You are such a piece of shit. I hate you.

DAD

I...

The sound of a kid crying. Show Dad leaning over the bed and the camera being dragged.

MOM

He's not filming this, is he? Dex, are you filming this? What are you doing under our bed? Honey, it's not what you think. Tell him.

DAD

It's not what you think. Now go to bed.

DEX

But...

DAD

BED. NOW.

Show how the movie stops and show Dex, now, hitting Delete. Show Dex going through the movies one by one. Delete, delete, delete. Delete, delete, delete.

Show Dex sleeping in his bed. Show how this was just a dream.

Show how Dad is on the phone with Mom, downstairs. Show him laughing. Show the brown birds hopping up and down on the kitchen floor. The laughing birds.

Show that.

Play a song that's hopeful. Show Dex smiling in his sleep.

CUT TO:

INT.—A GIRL'S BEDROOM

Show Tanis's bedroom. Tanis is lying on her bed, crying. Show that she is on the phone and Kate is on the other end. Understanding, giant-hearted Kate.

KATE

Dex Pratt is not worth this, sweetie.
He really isn't. He's a jerk.

TANIS

(sniveling)
I know. I think I love him though.

KATE

(sighing)
You don't love him. He's an asshole.
I've got to go; T's beeping in.

TANIS

Tell him Dex is an asshole.

KATE

I'm pretty sure he already knows that.

Show Tanis falling asleep. Pan her walls with all their numbers, codes that unlock everything or nothing. Show how she has drawn lines down all the models' faces and attached sticky notes of calculations.

Show her face. Draw numbers on there. The numbers are wrong. Show how the numbers are wrong.

Show Dex, now fully awake, writing the first email that he's written in forever. His hands feel funny on the keyboard. Show him flexing his fingers, like he's doing something that doesn't quite fit. Show how he's going to write something perfect and make it up to Tanis, make everything okay.

Show how instead, he googles Olivia. Show how she doesn't exist. No Facebook. No MySpace. No Twitter. No images. No news.

Nothing.

Show him googling Olivia's dad.

Show how he doesn't exist either.

Show Dex dragging his entire video collection to the trash.

Show Dex dragging one video back out again and then completely deleting the rest.

Show that Dex is still asleep.

Show that he isn't.

Show that he is making this up.

Then show that it is real.

CUT TO:

INT.—KITCHEN TABLE

Show Dad and his dollhouse, Glob asleep at his feet. Dad is whistling. Zoom in close on what looks like crumbs on the table. Show that the crumbs are really tiny brown birds. Show them shrinking away to nothing.

DEX

I could write the music.

FERAL

I'll play with you, man. We were great together.

DEX

Yeah, we coulda been contenders.

Show how Feral isn't there.

Pan the camera slowly around each room. Show how everyone is asleep. Dex. Tanis. Dad. Mom.

Show how Olivia is not asleep. Show her sitting upright in a bed. Staring into space. Fading in and out of focus.

chapter 19
september 25, this year.

The doctor says that my ACL is destroyed. No one is surprised, least of all me. He starts talking about surgery. I stop listening.

My dad and I are a fine pair, leaving the hospital. I use his chair like a walker, limping and pushing and leaning. He sits there, head bowed, like he can't imagine how we will get through this. Like this knee injury is the final thing, the thing we can't survive.

He is right.

When we get home, I've missed another day of school and there is something wrong with Glob. Something more than what is already wrong with Glob. I push Dad through the front door and Glob is right there in the hall, in the way. She is lying on her side. Her eyes are half open but her breathing is all wrong, hitching and catching and coming out in a rush, like a balloon popped.

"Now look what you've done," Dad says. Like it's my fault.

"Glob?" I say. "Good girl. Come here."

She doesn't move. She can't move. She's dying.

Dad leans forward and slides out of his chair and onto the floor until he's lying on the dog. He doesn't look at me, he's muttering, murmuring, gentle in a way that he never was.

"Glob," he says. "Glob."

I step over them as carefully as I can, which is hard when you can really only use one knee, although this stiff bandaging helps a lot. I go downstairs.

The basement of our house is full of grow equipment and stinks in spite of the fans that are meant to pump the stink outside where no one can smell it but the corn. I don't know how we haven't been caught. We must be draining the grid, all the power this sucks up. But maybe it's hidden by Our Joe's own use of power, his bank of greenhouses where he grows corn in the shoulder season. Early and late. He uses hydroponics too.

The plants in this crop look terrible. Gary's crop. A good crop is full of buds, healthy leaves, green lushness. It makes me think of jungles. I'm always expecting to see insects. This crop looks like skeletons, like what is left after everything rots away.

I know what to do, so I set about doing it. If you overlook what it is, it's sort of satisfying. For a few minutes, while I hunker down there under all those hot lights, I know what my dad felt like with the tomatoes.

It's totally different. I know it. But still.

I can hear Glob's nails scratching the wood floor upstairs. My dad's quiet voice.

I stay downstairs for a long time, and when I go up, the dog is not dead. Dad is back in his chair. Maybe I imagined the whole thing. Glob wags her tail weakly and drags herself over to her mat in the corner.

"How's it look?" says Dad, like nothing is different. Like he wasn't just lying on Glob in the hallway where Glob lay dying.

"Bad," I say. "But it's good stuff, it just doesn't *look* good. Looks aren't everything."

"Huh," says Dad. "I'd like to take a look."

"I already did it all," I tell him. "There's nothing to see. I gotta take a shower." I raise my hands and show him the dirt.

"Want to watch TV?" says Dad.

"Nah," I lie, "I have homework. And we have to eat too. I'll make something after I shower, okay?"

"Okay," he says. "Thanks," he adds. It's definitely an afterthought, but I'll take it.

"Sorry about your knee," he says. "Hurts?"

"Yeah," I say. "It's okay though."

"Okay." He nods. "Okay."

"Okay," I say.

And that's that.

In our old house, the family room was in a big open space, open to the kitchen. Here, everything is a tiny room, separate from everything else. I go into the tiny bathroom and blast the water, which comes out first icy cold and then boiling hot, there's nothing in between. I settle on cold and try to make the water wipe my brain clean so I don't have to think about anything at all.

I haven't done one bit of homework so far this year.

I want to rewind, start over, begin again.

Can you do that?

If I started over, I wonder if Olivia would exist.

chapter 20
september 26, this year.

I make it to school in plenty of time, and I sit on the steps and wait. I'm pretending that I'm just sitting here. I'm pretending that I'm not waiting for someone, but I am. I am waiting for Olivia. Because I'm crazy.

And high.

And I've forgotten if I want her to be real or not.

The first person I see is T-dot. I haven't seen him, not since the day of the knee. I don't know if he's been avoiding me or I've been avoiding him, but it doesn't really matter, does it?

"Hey," I go. "Man, I'm sorry. I was such a dick to you. Why do you put up with me?" I am so high that my tongue is sticking to my teeth and I'm lisping. Too much. It's hard to tell sometimes, until it's too late, and there you are, stuck on all the *s* words. *Thwap, thwap*. I laugh.

"Yeah," he says. He gives me a look. The look could say anything, but mostly it says, "Just say no to drugs." I pretend I don't see it. He sits down next to me. He's wearing brand-new shoes, and they glow white against the gray stairs. Seriously glow. Those shoes have haloes. I reach out to touch them and stop myself. "I don't really know," he says finally.

"Sorry," I say. "I don't know what's wrong with me." I shrug like it doesn't matter. His white shoes are in my peripheral vision, glowing.

"Something," he says. "There's *something* wrong with you."

"Yeah," I say. "I know. Did you talk to Kate? Did she say anything about Tanis? She hasn't talked to me for, like, days. I don't know." I squint up at the sun, like maybe it's written there, the number of days. Where are all the numbers? I'm losing track of time. It's sliding all around me like a slug's trail, sticking but slippery.

"She's pretty pissed," says T-dot. "You could try to be nice, you know? It's like, who the fuck are you? I don't think you're the same Dex Pratt. It's like aliens took over your body, you know?"

"Yeah," I go. "Well, they did."

"What?" he says. His face looms close. Pock marks. A cut where he shaved.

"I'm kidding," I say. I laugh. "I'm kidding. Fuck. You don't believe in that shit, do you?" I push him. I don't know why I do, but I do. Maybe I don't. But then I'm lying back on the stairs and they are biting into my back, and I look up and the sun blinds me and I think he's gone and all I can see is this rainbow of bright light around a face and it has to be him because it has his voice.

"Nah," he says. "But I heard that the new girl does."

"New girl?" I say, like I don't know exactly who he's talking about. I just want to hear him say her name. My heart speeds up. Faster, then faster. I hold my arm over my eyes to stop them from streaming. The light, you know.

"Olivia," he says.

"Oh, her." I shrug. My heart is going to burst out of me and gambol down the stairs like a baby deer. I sit up and I've got all those sun spots in my eyes that are making it hard to see anything. I look down at my shoes. They used to be white. I can't remember how long ago. Now they're gray. Sun spots. I can't see my hand. I go back to the shoes. There's a hole in the sole of the left one, where the rubber flaps down. "I've seen her around."

"She's hot, right?" he says. Or I think he does. "But she's totally cuckoo. Her dad's some kind of UFO expert or something, and she totally believes in it."

"Well," I say. "Well." I'm grinning. I try to stop grinning.

He's humming. Or someone is. Maybe it's me. Theme from *Star Wars* or some thing like that.

And then he's gone, and I'm alone on the stairs, humming.

Tanis walks right by me.

"Idiot," she hisses.

I grin. Nothing is terrible. Olivia is real and I am not crazy.

I want to shout it out loud. "Olivia is real and I am not crazy." I don't. I do.

I will myself to not feel the pain in my knee and a new pain coming from a lump on my head which must have been from the stairs. My ears are ringing. I drag myself to English, trailing behind Tanis as fast as I can.

My balls are itchy. There's no getting around it, it's true. It has nothing to do with anything, but it's kind of top of mind because I can't exactly jam my hand down my pants in the middle of English class. Mrs. D is droning on about who-knows-what and no one is listening because no one ever listens to Mrs. D.

I wish my balls weren't itchy.

I wish Olivia, who is real, would turn around and look at me. I've only barely just thought it when she does. She turns around. She winks. It's a wink that's caught by everyone around me. Tanis on my left. T-dot on my right. I mean, it has to be. They can't have missed it. Unless...

I keep my eyes straight ahead and then glance over at T. He shoots me a look.

"What?" I say. "*What?*"

Tanis is texting furiously, and then Kate is turning around and glaring at me too. I give up. I scratch my crotch vigorously. Fuck it. Who cares? Kate makes a gagging gesture. "Keep your pants on," she hisses. "God."

"Final essay," says Mrs. D, which makes me half listen because it's the second week of school and who is talking about final anything anyway? "Blah blah blah," she says.

I stare out the window. My knee is throbbing like it has its own heart, and not only that but it's actually having a heart attack at that exact moment. *Boom, boom, boom.* The leaves have just got the memo that it's fall and are all turning at once. The oak tree looks like it's caught fire overnight. The leaves are orange and red and brown, and it's really kind of amazing, if you're into that. It's another sunny day; the blue behind it makes my eyes ache.

Or my eyes ache because my eyes always ache.

Or something.

It's not good to be this high while you're at school. Shit happens. You lose control. I lose control. This usually doesn't happen to me, but today I...

I tilt sideways in my desk and concentrate on sitting straighter. Then I look like a guy who is trying to sit straight to hide something, so I slump back down again. The chair is killing my ass. My knee, my fucking knee. My other foot is tapping. I need to get out of here. T-dot reaches across the aisle and whacks my tapping leg with his pen. It hurts like a sting.

"Fuck!" I say, too loud.

Olivia tilts her head to the side suddenly, and her blond hair sweeps down and catches my eye and my breath catches in my chest, so I pretend I'm coughing and yawning at the same time. T-dot drums another song on his desk, and the drumming is in my skull and my pulse is skipping in the beat he dictates and my ears buzz. No, my phone buzzes. I can tell that it's Tanis without looking by the way her body tilts slightly toward mine. I look at her face before I read the screen. She gives me a crooked smile.

I'm relieved.

I read the text. *Still mad*, it says. But then there is a smiley. I hate smileys. I am relieved to see her smiley. Smileys make me feel like everyone is stupid. Tanis isn't stupid, but smileys are. I can't think this much about smileys. Saying "smileys" over and over again, even in my head, is making me grin in a way that I can't control, too much teeth. Don't laugh, I say to myself. No giggling.

Giggling is another one of those words.

I text back, *Okay, cool*. I text again, *U r pretty*. She smiles. A normal smile. Teeth managed. My lips are pulled back tight, too much gum showing. Stop thinking about smileys, I tell myself. Goddamn it. I bet Tanis flosses.

Tanis is wearing red cowboy boots. I watch her boots move around on the floor, and there is the sound of the hard soles on the linoleum that reminds me of dances. Tanis is good at things like dancing because she understands music from the inside out. She understands the beat. She says it's all the same: music and numbers and moving and standing still.

That isn't possible. I don't understand. How can moving be the same as standing still? The red boots tap an even rhythm, different from T-dot's drums, making them both as distracting as a dripping tap when you're trying to sleep, and I feel myself starting to jitter.

I'm not paying any attention at all to Mrs. D. I force myself to look up at her.

"Mr. Pratt," says Mrs. D. "Phone to me, please."

"What?" I say. "Why?"

"Because, Dexter, you were texting in class and, like I've just said six times while you've been staring at Miss Bowerman's feet, that is not allowed in my classroom."

"Oh," I say. "Shit. I mean, sorry."

Everyone laughs, but I wasn't trying to be funny. I hold up my phone. She shakes her head. I stand up and walk up to the front, phone in hand. As I walk by Olivia, she sticks something in my pocket. It's so fast, I almost don't notice.

I pull in my breath sharply. Who else noticed?

I look at Tanis. She's still giving me the half-grin.

"Anytime you're ready, Mr. Pratt," says Mrs. D. I hand her my phone and try to give her a charming smile, trying to keep the gums to a minimum. Too wolfish, I think. And I can tell she doesn't buy it. She shakes her head. Whatever Olivia put in my pocket is actually warm. I put my hand in my pocket, but I can't feel anything.

I sit down. My hand jammed in my pocket. Trying to feel.

T-dot raises his eyebrows at me. "What are you *doing*?" he says.

"Nothing," I say.

"Okay," says Mrs. D. She's shouting, so I know it isn't good. "Okay." She takes a deep breath. "Since Mr. Strait and Mr. Pratt don't feel they need to listen to the requirements for the final paper, I assume that means they are ready right now to pitch their ideas. Gentlemen?"

"Huh?" says T-dot. "What?"

The ripple of laughter around the classroom is nervous. Mrs. D glowers. "ENOUGH!" she shouts. She repeats it more quietly. "Enough."

"Boys," she says, "you'll give me your topics, now. It's ten thousand words. I'm sure you didn't hear that the first time. Ten thousand words on a topic of your choice.

And you better love what you pick because this is going to be the paper that matters more than any other paper you've ever written, *capisce*?"

"Yeah," says T-dot. He hardly even hesitates. "I'll write about swimming, man. No worries." He looks pretty pleased with himself.

My brain is blank.

What are my interests. Pot? Olivia? Being miserable? Movies?

I am no longer interested in movies.

I have quit the movie business.

I was never in the movie business.

My head throbs.

"I don't know," I say.

"I'm waiting, Mr. Pratt," she sighs. "Ten seconds, and then Mr. Strait here gets to pick for you."

I have nothing to say. The room is frozen in a diorama. I feel like I'm holding it all in my hand, in miniature, my mouth half open, no one talking, nothing, and I'm in control of that. "Wellll...," I say.

T-dot coughs. "Drugs," he murmurs.

"ALIENS!" I shout. "Like, you know. Something. I don't know. Yeah. Aliens."

"Done," says Mrs. D.

And that's that. The bell goes and the class spills out the door like liquid mercury, scattering in the hallway into a million tiny droplets of silver, splitting and multiplying and splitting until there are so many people I feel like I've disappeared.

The thing in my pocket is a small orange stone. It is perfectly smooth. It is tinged with blue.

I don't get it.

I spend all of my lunch hour looking for Olivia, but she's nowhere. I look everywhere. She's just gone.

chapter 21
september 26, evening.

You aren't going to believe me, but when it happens, the last thing that I am thinking about is aliens. That's the truth.

I am in the corn.

And...

I am in the corn and I am high and the movie starts. I am not directing this movie.

It happens.

There are aliens.

Listen.

There was a vortex.

The taste of pennies and dog hair.

Plate-sized eyes.

It *happens*.

What kind of sick fuck would make that up?

Real.

Not real.

I am there and then I'm not. And then I'm nowhere and everywhere, and it is a vacuum and I'm spinning and there is a hand in my knee and...

And...

And.

You want me to tell you that I made it up, but I didn't.

Look at my knee. You can't make that up.

You can't make any of this shit up. All of it is real.

All of it.

Sometimes I think there's a kind of a hitch, and the difference between what is real and what isn't becomes like one of those sun spots I saw this morning. It's not really a black spot, is it? It's something else. I just don't know exactly what.

Sometimes there is proof: an orange stone, a cured knee.

Sometimes there are just your memories competing.

I just remembered something about that day when I learned to swim. I just remembered how, after being patient all day, Dad threw me in like a stick for a dog. He threw me. The water was over my head and it was darker than any room could ever be. I remember how the weeds tangled around my arms and legs and when I opened my eyes, all I could see was black liquid and death.

I remember how I fought my way up.

I remember how he was proud of that.

I don't know why I'm telling you this right now.

There were fucking *aliens* and my knee was fucking *cured*. That should trump everything else, real or imagined, remembered or forgotten.

There was something about the whiteness, which was the opposite of the blackness of that water on that day. There was something about the air that was liquid, and I am losing my shit and I am losing my shit and I am losing my shit and I am losing my self.

Was it real?

No?

You tell me. Someone tell me, goddamn it.

Please.

chapter 22

"Where were you?" Dad says when I finally stumble inside. No time has passed. All the time has passed. Enough time has passed that species have become extinct and been reborn.

I want to cry. I want so fucking much to cry.

Why can't I cry?

"Nowhere," I say.

My brain keeps ticking over a slide show of disconnected images:

I am carrying a tray of glasses made of thin crystal and the wind going over the tray makes a sound of whistling.

In black and white, I am disappearing.

There is a bowl of fruit.

My dad is a dog. The dog is dead. The dog is dying.

I am alone.

I am the dog.

I am dying.

I think maybe I faint, I don't know.

I open my eyes and I'm on the floor in the front hall and Dad is looking down on me, confused.

"I'm okay," I lie.

My dad is asking me something.

"Where were you?" he says again. He doesn't sound mad, but then again, I can tell by his flat affect and the way he's holding his hands extra carefully, like a drunk trying to walk a straight line, that he's taken an extra something from his vast array of *somethings*.

"Uh," I say, "I got dizzy."

I glance at the clock. Again.

"Are you high?" he says. Then, "Christ, answer me. Your eyes are red as hell."

He rolls over to the kitchen table. He is behind the house he is building. The house stands between me and him. There are people in the window of his house. A boy and a girl.

There are people in between us. Those people are us. We are in between us.

My brain is screaming. There is a Tilt-A-Whirl and I want to get off.

I shift from foot to foot to foot and I'm rocking like a little kid, and he pulls his magnifying lens back down over his eyes. I haven't seen this house before. It's new. Did he do all this today? It is nearly complete, with gingerbread trim and detailed siding. His big saw is out in the living room. Did Gary bring it up or has it always been in the living room?

I am still dizzy, or dizzy again.

Plate-sized eyes. A hand on my knee.

Come on. Make it goddamn stop.

I grab the doorframe to stop myself from tumbling headfirst onto the table. I feel funny, bad, strange. Like I've got amnesia but not enough to make me forget, just enough to make everything look slightly strange and unfamiliar. Wrong. Out of place. A film that's offset from its soundtrack, the mouths moving faster than the words can be heard. The feeling you sometimes get when you fall asleep too fast, too deep and are startled awake and it seems like the walls of the house shifted while you were dreaming.

Dad coughs. "Like it?" he says. He points at his construction. The dollhouse is tiny, too tiny to *even be* a dollhouse. It's just a tiny house. Tiny stairs and tiny windows. Tiny doors and tiny people. His dollhouses always come with a family, did I mention that? Father, mother, brother, sister, dog.

Like we used to be.

He looks at me, expectantly.

I shrug. I'm still feeling like I can't get a breath all the way in. I'm so tilted inside, the room feels like it's shifting away from me. I'm sick, that's all.

My memories are tiny. I am tiny.

I want to tell him what just happened.

But what did just happen?

I don't want to tell him.

Can't tell him.

What would he do? "Dad, I think that I was just abducted by aliens in the cornfield." I don't think he could take it.

I can't take it.

But this is my goddamn problem.

This is *my* crazy.

It's a cry for help, I tell myself. I'm just asking for attention.

I don't tell him.

He looks so old, squinting through his half-glasses at the tiny toilet he's cradling in his hand like it's a precious gem, pretending to care about where I've been.

"I actually was just running," I say firmly, forcing my voice to be strong.

"Running," he repeats. "What are you playing at?" He turns around and stares right at me. "You can hardly walk," he says finally. "I'd think even you could come up with a better lie than that. Just how baked are you?"

I can't answer that because I am baked. Can you measure bakedness? I want to answer him, give him a number like Tanis would. "Seven." Or "Eight thousand." What measurement would I use? Miles? Pounds?

I am always baked.

I cannot remember not being baked.

The entire time I have been back home, I have been one-hundred-percent high, one hundred percent of the time. Two hundred and fifty percent. "Any percent higher than one hundred is just stupid," says Tanis. But Tanis isn't here, so I guess she says it in my head or has said it enough that it echoes there.

"Baked," I say. Maybe it sounds like agreement or an admission of guilt, but I don't care. The eyes were like quicksand and pulled me inside. Can you ever explain that to a person?

"How baked?" he says again.

"Yeah," I say. "Well, I don't know, Dad. I think...my knee. It's better."

He takes off his glasses and gives me a look. A look that says, "Yeah, right."

"I'm serious, Dad," I say. "Look at it."

I stand next to him, so close I can smell his unwashed stink. Urine and cigarette smoke and whiskey and that dusty tang of medicine, the salt of sweat.

I pull my pant leg up, half expecting to see it like it has been—swollen, purple streaks down the sides—half knowing it is going to look fine. We both peer at it, like it's a specimen of something under glass. The knee looks totally normal. Knobbly, hairy.

"Huh," he says. "That's..."

"Yeah," I say. "It is. A miracle, I guess. You want dinner?"

"What the hell," he says, scratching his head. "What the *hell*?"

I shrug. "You want dinner or not?" I swallow. The spinning of the room is slowing. My mouth tastes like I've been sucking a sockful of rusty nails but I am okay.

"I am okay," I say out loud, and it seems to bounce around the room like something silver and shiny that we both watch for a few minutes, mesmerized.

There's a long pause. He's looking at me like I'm a mosquito who has suddenly learned how to perform a guitar solo. Finally: "You cooking?" he asks.

"Sure," I tell him.

Tonight I'm going to make meatballs. We can have meatball subs and a big green salad with our corn tonight. I'm ravenous. I need to eat. I need to eat everything. I roll up my sleeves. My arms are still shaking a bit. Not so much that Dad notices, but enough that I leave the room fast before he does.

"Nice dollhouse," I say over my shoulder from the doorway.

"It is, isn't it?" he says. "She's a beauty. This may be my best one yet. I'm thinking yellow. Or taupe. But...she seems to want to be yellow. Do you think?"

"Yellow's nice," I say. "I like yellow."

Our old house was yellow. Mom used to say that yellow houses held on to only happy memories. She also said that no monsters ever lived in yellow houses.

Of course, my mom turned out to be full of shit.

Right before she left, she went down to the basement and she took all those glass jars of tomatoes that she'd worked so hard to preserve. Dozens and dozens and dozens of them. She took them and she stood on the stairs and, one by one, she smashed them on the cement floor.

When I came home, it looked like a sea of blood. I was only fourteen and I'd just seen *Texas Chainsaw Massacre*. I thought someone had been killed.

Who does that to their kid?

Happy memories, my ass.

I wonder if he'll add that detail. A basement flooded with red, like the house itself was hemorrhaging from the inside out.

My dad does okay selling his houses, but I don't know why he bothers. In his best month, he made six hundred dollars selling them online. We make that in a week selling pot, sometimes ten times that. But he likes to think that other people think that the houses are carrying us.

I slowly take vegetables from the fridge and line them up on the counter. I reach for the knife and I wonder who will defend Dad in court when we get caught. In the divorce, Dad represented himself and lost badly. Mack Wong represented Mom, and now Mack is my dad's archenemy. But he's also the only other lawyer in town.

I guess I have to just hope we don't get caught.

But I know we will. It's just a matter of time.

The blade on this knife has been sharpened so many times that it's lost its shape. The edge is so sharp, it's paper thin and cuts into the cutting board like a razor.

Dad goes back to his work, and I chop up an onion and I think about how I read somewhere that Tibetan monks can control their heartbeats. I am not a Tibetan monk. My heart is going so fast, with no sign of slowing down, and yet it's not scaring me. It feels normal, a thousand birds in my chest flapping their wings. I slowly mush the onion into the meat with an egg and some bread crumbs. I look out the window. *Aliens*. I think about how the smell permeated everything, how it permeated me. I can still smell it.

It happened. Or it didn't.

Did it?

"No," I say. I pound my fist hard onto the countertop.

"You okay?" calls Dad.

"Yeah," I say.

"You cut yourself or something?"

"No, Dad. Sorry," I say.

The sky is alive with stars, but nothing up there is moving. No flashing lights. No indication that what happened was real. My thoughts slow to a jog, like pigs wading through mud. I feel like I'm dreaming. Still. Again.

The window starts to steam up.

Through the condensation, all I can see are shadows and the distant lights of houses, the neon sign of the Motel 6 at the exit from the freeway. The headlights are so far away that they are just dots, shrinking and vanishing over the foothills.

Dots of light everywhere.

Those dots of light in the sky that I thought were stars: Are they? Is one of those dots moving away? Or moving toward? What else is there that we can't see?

I put the meatballs into the fry pan and they sizzle and spit, droplets of hot grease bouncing out and hailing onto my forearms, a tiny hailstorm of pain.

"Smells good," Dad calls.

"Thanks," I say. "Yeah, it does."

I'm starving. I could reach into the hot oil and eat one half raw. That's how empty I am. I am completely empty. There is nothing in me, except my heart, racing in a hollow space.

The pot of water for the corn bubbles and I go about making the salad. Chopping lettuce, tomatoes, radishes, cucumber. That's one thing about living on Our Joe's farm, we get food. Apart from corn, corn and more corn, he has a vegetable garden that's just for us and him. Well, just for him, I think, but I take what Dad and I need.

I have to. Someone has to look after us, and it sure isn't going to be the man with the miniature kitchen sink clamped between his lips. He puts the sink into the hole in the counter. Then he is painting a dish to look dirty. Two dishes. Three. He breaks a dish in half and puts it on the floor.

"Dad," I say, but he doesn't hear me.

Carefully, he cuts some of Glob's hair into tiny strands and spreads them on the couch. It looks like he's smiling, but it could just be a squint.

chapter 23
september 27, this year.

In the morning, I wake up with a pounding headache, and I don't light up because I'm scared to. And I am never scared. Not like this. I make myself shower and get dressed by saying it out loud, like a goddamn crazy person.

"Shower and get dressed," I say. "Fuck you," I add.

I have not had a shower and got dressed without lighting up for so long that I don't know. I don't know anymore when I started or how to stop or why I do anything that I do. And trying to think of when or why makes me think of the chicken and the egg, how one of them came first. But also how it's more complicated than that. A chicken-like bird laid a regular chicken-like bird egg, but inside *that* egg was a slightly altered chicken-like bird and gradually it became a chicken. What was in the egg of that dinosaur bird? So fuck it, nothing came first.

My hands feel empty and strange, like a creepy marionette in a horror movie, only this marionette's hands are shaking too hard to be believed. I watch my shaking hands try to take out the ring in my ear but they can't land on the ear. They are bees, trying to land on a flower in a windstorm. The ear moves. My head moves. I move my head. Which came first? I need a smoke.

"Get dressed," I say to my ugly goddamn reflection. "Put on your shirt." But I can't. I can't button it. The buttons move and shift. The buttons are moths and they fly away. I throw it on the floor and put on a T-shirt instead. The T-shirt stinks.

I take it off.

I put on a sweater. I never wear sweaters. Is this even my sweater? The sweater is black and soft and has holes down the side, small perfect circles, and I don't care. It doesn't stink. I'm hot but shaking, cold but sweating, I don't know what I am. Whose sweater is this?

I go downstairs. I go back upstairs and change the stranger's sweater back into a shirt that is mine—a white shirt, an old St. Joe's school shirt—and I feel like someone else in it. It settles cold against my skin and I'm instantly clammy.

"Get it together," I say to myself. I hold my hands as still as I can and move fast, jam a stretcher in my ear, pulling so it hurts. "Fucking get it together." I can hear Dad wheeling around the living room. Glob's half-hearted morning bark that says, "Feed me already."

I go downstairs.

"Morning," I say. The shirt feels tight around my neck. I unbutton another button. Why am I so nervous?

"It is," says Dad. "It *is* morning." He is shaking pills into his hand. *Rattle, rattle*. The sound hurts my ears. There is something wrong and I don't know what it is. I know what it is but I can't put my finger on it. There is something that I know. My knee feels too smooth, like it's full of oil, like it's going to slip right off, my leg bending backward, my body falling to the floor.

I throw bread in the toaster and wait, watching, and suddenly it's burning. The fire alarm goes off and I bang it with a broom handle until it stops. I go to open the kitchen window.

I open the kitchen window and something inside my head splits open, and open again, and layers of it open and open and open like paper unfolding.

I open the kitchen window and I shout. Glob is barking. Dad is dropping his pills. The alarm starts up again. There is so much noise.

And...

And.

And there *it* is, laid out before me in the half-light of the dawn, sprawling across the acres of corn. The dew makes it sparkle, makes it even more surreal than it is. Circles and lines, a pattern so huge that I cannot see where it ends or where it begins.

I cannot possibly be making this up.

For a second, I think I'm going to faint again, and then my phone beeps on the counter. I pick it up out of habit sort of and partly out of relief that I have to look at something else. It's Tanis.

Wrecked my back bad last night, it says. There's a sad smiley.

Feel better, I type with one hand. I start to type more and then I backspace, key by key, over the words *CROP* and *CIRCLE*.

"Dad," I say. It comes out like a croak. "DAD!" I yell louder.

"What is it?" he asks. "Can you help me pick these up?" His wheels are crushing the pills into dust. "Can you help me?" He sounds panicked. "Son," he says.

"Come here," I say.

"Whatever it is," he says, "you bring it to me."

"Dad," I say, "I can't exactly do that."

I guess there is something about the tone in my voice that gets him to finally pay attention. He wheels over, bumping his fingers on the doorframe. His knuckles are already scarred from that, and there is a dark stain on the wood at that level. I should help him, but I can't move.

I'm holding on to my phone and staring out the window. He rolls up behind me too quickly and the phone falls on the floor and the battery cover pops off.

"Now I've done it," Dad says. "Sorry. I've busted it."

"Dad," I say, "I don't give a shit about the phone. LOOK OUTSIDE."

He wheels up to the window, which is his only vantage point without counter and sink in his way. He doesn't say anything. I watch his face.

Finally, "You do that?" he asks.

"What?" I go.

"Did. You. Do. That?" he enunciates, like I'm deaf or an idiot.

"Dad," I say, "don't be *insane*. How could I *do* that? It's...huge. It would be impossible. I didn't do it. I think... it was...aliens."

My voice is going up and down like the lines on a polygraph. And I say it again, "How would I do that?" I feel like I'm lying, and I wonder if I am and I've forgotten what I know and what I don't know.

Do I know something?

He laughs, a short, sharp bark of a laugh. "Aliens," he repeats. "My sorry ass, aliens did that. More likely Our Joe needs to make a mortgage payment."

I look at him to see if he's kidding. He's not kidding. He does not think it's real. Which is okay, because I don't either.

Only I know that it is. I can't tell him that it is. For one thing, he won't believe me.

I also know that it isn't. There is something.

Okay, there is more than something.

I recognize that shape. The shape is not a crop circle shape. It's a Celtic knot. It means...

I know that Celtic knot.

"Live," I say out loud. And I remember without wanting to remember, like someone is grabbing my brain and forcing it to crank backward into the summer.

"No," I say. But fuck me, right? *Whoosh*, I fall backward through time, tripping and falling and sick, and I'm at the lake and we, all four, are lying on a blanket, head-to-head, bodies pointing outward like the arrows on a compass, and T-dot is saying, "We need a motto."

"A motto?" Tanis says. "Like what, 'All for one and one for all'?"

"Yeah," I say, "but not stupid."

"Fuck you," she says.

"Hey," says Kate. "Stop."

"Something shorter," says Tanis. "Something that's like a word with two meanings. Something that means something to us."

We are all lying there, and the sun is so hot on my skin. And I like how it feels, like I can hardly stand it, but I'm not moving. Like I know I'm burning but I don't care, like how moths feel when they die in a candle flame. My eyes are closed and they keep talking and I feel like I should have the answer, but I can't be bothered. Why do we need a motto anyway? Are we some kind of fucked-up club? But I say that part out loud, and Kate says, "Yeah, it's sort of a club. I guess. Right? It's like we are all in this thing together."

"In what thing?" I say. I stand up. The ground is gravelly under my feet, hard-packed, too dry. I want to dive into the lake. My skin is burning. "Life? We're in life together?"

"Haven't you been listening?" Kate says. She hates me so much. And I have been listening, but I also don't know what she's talking about. It's like I listen and nothing sticks. The words are oil and I'm water and they float somewhere above me. And I don't give a fuck. I dive into the lake, and when I come out, Tanis says, "We decided."

I say, "What?"

And she says, "Live."

"What are you talking about?" I say.

"Our motto," she says. "Our word. Like a code, right?"

"Okay," I say. I shrug. I lie down again on the blanket and the sun instantly evaporates the water and I am my own steam room, lying there in the heat, and they are talking but I am not listening.

"Live," I say out loud, now in the kitchen, and in my head, my hand reaches out and traces the tattoo on Tanis's back. The knot, the goddamn knot. My phone beeps, and I pick it up and on the screen, all caps: *LIVE*.

From Kate. Who doesn't text me.

Then another, from Tanis.

Then T-dot.

The air in the room is gone and I am breathing molten metal, and I am trying to remember something that is gone again, fleeting as the rainbow reflecting on the wall behind me, the sun hitting the glass at just a certain angle for only a second.

"Better take a picture," Dad says, jolting me out of my reverie. "I guess it didn't break after all." He nods at my phone on the floor. The battery casing has fallen off but it seems to be working.

I pick it up in slow motion. Snap the cover back in place.

I point the phone's camera lens out the window and take a picture. Something inside me knots and unknots. I wish I had my real camera. I want to film something. I need to film myself seeing this and remembering, but I am not high enough. I need to be high. Not being high is a mistake.

My brain has the pieces of a puzzle and refuses to stick them back together. And I can't think about anything but going upstairs for a puff. Because. Because. Because.

When I'm smoking, I understand things. There is something here I need to understand.

"Our Joe," my dad says. "What a crazy fucker, he is. Who does this? He's probably going to somehow turn this into a sideshow. I'm calling him."

"He didn't do it," I say, but Dad can't hear me because he's already gone.

He wheels himself back down the hall and picks up the old-fashioned dial phone. I hear the numbers whirring by slowly, as if they are a million miles away. I turn and go upstairs. The view is better from there.

Live.

Live?

"That's just all there is," Tanis said that day at the lake. "It's like...enough. LIVE. That's all I want. I just want to live. I'm going to live my life, you're going to live your life and we're going to live, in spite of...you know. You know, Dex, I know you know. It's just enough. For us. To just live. Our way. Don't you see?"

I nodded. I rolled over onto her and her skin was so hot from the sun and mine was so cold, I swear to God, it fucking sizzled. And then...

Well.

I was in the cornfield, and then it was bright and I wasn't. And my knee was fucked up and now it isn't. And...

And.

I stare at the flattened corn. The curves look like they've been cut into the ground with a laser. What kind of aliens would copy my girlfriend's tattoo?

No aliens.

Because there are no aliens.

There is only me. And Tanis. T-dot. And Kate.

I can hear my dad shouting something into the phone or at me, I can't tell which.

"I'm coming," I yell.

I take one last look out the window before I go back down the stairs. I feel something like pride. Or maybe it's panic.

I lie down on my bed and smoke and smoke. I smoke until the haze in my room looks yellow and the light changes and Dad has stopped calling me and I have missed Math! And Bio! And Everything Else! And maybe I fall asleep and wake up and fall asleep and dream that giant Transformers are moving slowly through the cornfield, *stomp, stomp*, a robot army, and in their massive footprints I find flocks of dead birds, squashed into the dirt, and I wake up feeling sick and upside down and like I'm drowning. I get up. The spit in my mouth is paste-thick and I spit into the laundry basket. There are voices downstairs. Gary, I guess. Dad. Someone else.

I go down. I go downstairs and there they are in the kitchen, Dad and Gary and Our Joe, all looking out the window like they are waiting for something to happen. I croak a greeting, grab a glass of water and gulp it down. Then another.

"Dry in here," Gary says sarcastically, and I glower at him.

"Dex," says Our Joe. He nods at me like I have something to say, which I don't.

I grunt.

Dad says, "A mystery."

"I don't care what it is," says Our Joe. "As far as I'm concerned, it's a gift from God."

He has the big red nose of a chronic alcoholic, but he doesn't drink. He says he's allergic to corn and maybe that's true. He sniffs exuberantly and rubs his hands together.

"God," he says. "THANK YOU. Time to cash out and retire."

"I don't think God had much to do with it," I say. My heart is pounding in my ears and I still can't figure out why I'm scared. Not really. Our Joe is tiny. I never noticed before how short he was. He always seemed so much larger than life. I can see wax in his ear. Smell the stale stink of his armpits.

"Son," he says, "I don't care who *did* it, I'm just thrilled as peach pie to see it."

"Aliens," I say and take another swallow of water, which tastes like chemicals. I cough. Cough and cough.

"God gave us the aliens then," says Our Joe. "God just gave Our Joe a big ol' paycheck, that's for damn sure." He smashes me hard on the back, like he's saving me from choking, but I wasn't choking. I want to punch him back, and I almost do, but then I stop. I think, You'll get what's coming to you. Or maybe I say it. I say, "You'll get what's coming to you." And Dad says, "Dex," a warning in his voice like a dog's growl or maybe Glob is growling. And I shrug and pretend I don't care or I don't know, and all the sounds are coming from the wrong sources, echoing in the room.

"Gotta get goin'," Gary says, like anyone cares.

"See ya," I say. I can't help but notice that Dad doesn't say anything, and Gary stomps out, heavily, like a kid having a tantrum. I drink another glass of water. How much water can I drink? I need more, but Dad is staring and I'm suddenly self-conscious. I put the glass on the counter, too hard. It cracks.

"Did you do it, Joe?" Dad asks.

"I didn't," says Our Joe. "I would have if I could have, but I sure didn't. Oh good, here they are."

And I can see a small group of cars, coming down the driveway. *Channel 6 News*. I swallow. Something is starting and I can't help but feel like I got this ball rolling, but I have no idea how or why. And I'm so tired. I'm really tired. I just want to go to sleep and maybe save those poor fucking birds.

I go upstairs and lie down, but I can't sleep. My legs are restless, and Tanis and T-dot keep calling and I don't answer. I lie on my bed. I stare at my ceiling and the old posters and listen to Dad rolling around downstairs and Glob's claws on the wood floors and noise drifting in through the window.

By nightfall, helicopters are circling overhead and THC rolls through my body and smoothes everything out and leaves me feeling empty and full and light and meaningless and slow and fuck it, who cares?

Not me.

I turn on the TV just to have something else to look at, and *CBC Newsworld* is showing a constant streaming video of the field. Our field. Experts are weighing in, their voices like mosquitoes buzzing in my ear. There are experts in this? There are experts in everything. Somewhere in the world is an expert on me, and I hope someone calls him in soon and asks him, "What went wrong?"

"Crop circles and Celtic knots are different patterns," one is saying. "Not authentic."

And I think, You fucking idiot. What's an *authentic* crop circle? That's like an *authentic* alien abduction. Then I think, Wait. I stand up and go to my window. I have binoculars. I don't know why I have them. With the binoculars, I can see who is who. I can see lots of kids from school. I see Tanis's dad. I see that Our Joe has set up what looks like a T-shirt booth and he's selling something. How did he get T-shirts ready so quickly? I see my dad.

My dad is at the end of the ramp, watching. Glob gets up every few minutes and barks.

Where am I in all this?

"Live," I say out loud.

My phone beeps. Tanis again. *Am coming to CU*, it says.

I stand up and look at myself in the mirror. I look bad: bedhead and yesterday's dirt. I smell worse.

I rub my T-shirt over my pits, spray on some shit body spray and put on a fresh shirt. I look in the mirror. "You reflect poorly," I say. "On me." My eyes are red. I laugh without smiling. I am a robot. I am a Transformer. I am crushing small brown birds as I walk around my room.

My room moves around me like an amoeba and sucks me in. I grab hold of the bed.

Who are you anyway?

"Stop," I tell myself. I change my ear stretcher so I'm forced to focus on something small. When the stretcher itself is out, my ear hole gapes like a toothless woman yawning.

I go downstairs. The stairs creak. My feet are balloons and they aren't properly attached to my body and I am floating. In the air, the dust mites are multicolored miniature rainbows. When I push the screen door open and gulp in some cooling fresh air, I'm shocked to see a woman sitting in the mouse chair, which is this disgusting, old, rotten, purple-velvet monstrosity that we never bothered to move off the porch. She looks surprised to see me, too, but she gathers herself and hoists herself up. It's the kind of chair you can get stuck in. I don't reach out and help. The woman has a funny look in her eye, like she knows something. She has TV hair. No one in real life has hair like that.

"Can I help you?" I say.

"Yes," she says. "Are you Dexter Pratt?"

"Dex," I correct her. Her hand is outstretched, so I take it and let go, like a hand clench instead of a shake. Her skin is as smooth as wax. She looks like one of those Japanese blow-up dolls. Immediately she is naked and my mouth is on…

Wait. *Cut*. Fuck it. What am I doing? I wish hard that I had my camera pointed at her, giving me distance. But this is real, not an imagining.

"Sorry," I say, even though she can't know what I'm talking about. She looks puzzled, shrugs.

I'm blushing. Stop it, I tell myself. Stop it.

Just then, a guy pops up from behind the rhododendron. *He* has a huge camera, with a dazzling light on a pole. Everything is phallic and hilarious, and I giggle. I try to stop but it keeps coming. I swallow hard. My brain provides the word *smiley*, and right away I smile too big.

"I'm Christy O'Leary, *Channel Four News*," she says brightly into the lens. "Here today with Dex Pratt, who lives in the house on the site of the largest crop circle ever seen, and the first to feature a word. Dex," she says, turning to me, "what do you have to say about all this?"

"Uh," I say because I'm a fucking genius with words. "Um."

"Do you think, like experts are saying, that this is an elaborate hoax?" She laughs throatily. "And where were YOU last night?"

"I...," I go. "I don't know. It's pretty big to be a hoax."

"So you're voting for the aliens!" She laughs gaily. "Score one for the green guys!"

The light abruptly goes off and before I can say anything, Christy O'Leary is gone, sweeping down the ramp like she's walking the catwalk on TV, her heels sinking into the stinking ground.

I slump down into the chair.

I close my eyes. My lungs are wings that are trying to lift me up. I breathe in and in and they flap and spread.

"Fly," I say.

When I open my eyes, Tanis is standing in front of me, arms crossed, tapping her toe. She's wearing pink sneakers covered with skulls, and jeans so tight it looks like she's just dipped her legs in blue paint.

"Well?" she says. "This is great. I mean, it's working." She leans into me and then onto me, and she's too heavy. I can't breathe. "It's scary but it isn't. Right?"

I push her off. "Why are you so happy?" I say. "I thought your back was messed up."

"It is," she says. "But it feels better. Anyway, I'm happy. Because it's perfect," she says. "Pro. Por. Tion." She enunciates. "Perfect. It's so beautiful." She smiles. There are freckles of light on her pupils. She sparks. I blink. She reaches into her pocket and pulls out a photo that she's rolled up into a tube. She's almost reverential as she unrolls it. "Perfect," she says. "No one would ever believe that humans did that."

"Maybe they didn't," I say.

She laughs. Cocks her head to the side. "Dex," she says. She stops laughing. "Dex," she says, "don't you...?"

"What?" I say.

She keeps talking. She has the accent of a small town. Sloping vowels. An "eh" she can't drop. But either I can't hear her or she's speaking in code. A blur hovers in the air between us. There is a starburst of white light behind her head, like the corn itself is sparking, reflecting what she is saying.

"I...," I start to say. "I have a goddamn migraine or something."

She puts her lips against mine. "Be okay," she says. "Dex..."

"Forget it," I say. I push her away.

I get up and sprint down the ramp so fast I know she can't keep up. Then I am running for real. I run into the sea of flashbulbs. It's like diving underwater, dazzling and suffocating, both. I run through them. I am swimming. I am holding my breath so I don't drown.

My whole life, I've always been so fucking afraid of drowning.

chapter 24
september 28, this year.

There's a TV show on in the middle of the morning, on one of those public channels with no ads. It's a kids' show about art. There's a British host who is a bit too sure of himself. He has a British way of lilting that grates. I lie on my bed, which is still soaking wet from the sweat of my bad dreams, and watch him. He makes art from a piece of plastic wrap. He paints things. The product at the end looks impossible. He paints shadows with black and some kind of tea.

At the end of the episode, he grabs a bag of vegetables and sports equipment. He starts laying them down on the ground in an empty parking lot. He tosses cabbages here, a tennis net there, a handful of badminton birdies and three ears of corn.

The camera pans further and further out. It's a dragon. The dragon is pouring fire from his mouth. A knight is aiming a sword at his heart.

It's a pile of cabbage and corn.

Outside, the sounds of people are like the buzz of insects in my ears, and suddenly something falls into place and makes sense and I gasp.

I want to call my mom.

I call my mom. I watch my fingers dialing her number in Vancouver, the drag of my finger past the one. The six. The zero. The four.

I hang up.

Whatever I was thinking slips away, leaving me feeling confused. I go outside. I want a goddamn hot chocolate. I want a T-shirt. I grab some money and make my way to Our Joe. I give him my money. The chocolate tastes like chalk on my tongue. The T-shirt smells like warehouse dust. When did he get these printed up? I wonder. When did he have time?

I'm missing something. It's like I have all the facts but nothing fits.

I don't have all the facts.

I *had* the facts, but I lost them.

The facts are fish and they are silver and tiny and they are swimming back up into the sky like a reverse rain.

I go closer and closer to the crowd. What is a crowd? There are maybe fifty people here. It seems like a lot. There is some kind of platform. I don't know where that came from. Raised up, so the crowd is all in one place, staring down at our field, and I think about the dirt and how it feels when you press your face into it, damp and real.

I go closer and closer. I am looking for someone. And you know exactly who I'm looking for if you've been following along. Because I haven't seen her for days and the orange stone is still in my pocket and I don't know why.

I look and look, as if looking for her will put her there in the scene where she isn't. And then she is.

So it worked.

A flash of Olivia's hair, and then I see her jacket. I see her hand gesturing. I see her step down from the platform. I see her turn to look at me, directly at me. I see her disappear into the corn. I want to follow her. I dump my hot chocolate on the ground and jam the T-shirt on inside out. I want to follow her, but I don't.

I can't.

The people on the platform are staring at me.

I go back to the house.

I wish I didn't feel so strange.

I sit in the mouse chair and smoke another spliff. Just one more. Just one more before.

chapter 25

EXT.—CORNFIELD—NIGHT TIME

And...

SCENE:

It's dark and the stars are out. Pan the sky slowly, showing the stars. The sky is big here. Somehow demonstrate how the sky is bigger here than in other places. Show the sky in Vancouver for contrast. There are no stars. The stars are there, but you cannot see them.

There is a difference between something being absent and something being invisible. Take note of that. It could make a difference.

Show how the corn makes shadows in the dark.

Let the silence play. No soundtrack. Then the sound of breathing and shuffling feet. Then giggling.

Definitely giggling.

Pull the camera out far and then farther and then farther still. Use some kind of a crane. Get so far up you can see the house at the end with the lights glowing. From far away, you can't see the cracked windows and moss on the roof.

Zoom in to show that.

Zoom out again. Make it so silent you can hear the camera buttons being pressed.

If there were buttons.

Which there aren't.

TANIS

All you have to do is follow the map in your hand.

KATE

But how does it make sense? Our footsteps are all different sizes.

T-DOT

This isn't going to work. I can't do this.

TANIS

You have to do this. We agreed.

T-DOT

If I go to jail, I blow my scholarship.

TANIS

Todd, don't be an asshole.

KATE

I don't know, Tan. This seems…far-fetched.

TANIS

Everything is far-fetched. Just do it, okay?

Go back to silence.

Zoom in on Dex Pratt. Dex thinks he is alone in a cornfield. Somehow show that he thinks he is alone. Show that Dex is high.

DEX

What the fuck?

Show the crisscrossing of headlights, passing over Dex. Show Dex rolling to avoid being crushed. Show that.

Add a soundtrack. It needs to be the kind of music you get lost in, loud, thrashing music that negates your ability to think anything else.

Show the cornstalks in the moonlight.

Show the stillness.

Zoom the camera out and show the crop circle, perfectly formed.

Show how the pattern is a Celtic knot with no beginning or no end.

CUT TO:

INT.—DEX'S BEDROOM

Show Dex and Tanis. Show that they are naked. Zoom in tight on the tattoo on Tanis's back.

A Celtic knot.

With no beginning and no end.

CUT BACK TO:

Dex Pratt running through the corn. The soundtrack so loud now, it's impossible to make out what song is playing.

And...

CUT.

Delete scene.

It doesn't make sense.

Undelete the scene. Wait until you can think of a way to make it come together.

Delete it.

You will never know.

Undelete.

Delete.

Add a voice-over. Have Captain Obvious announce the obvious thing that Dex Pratt cannot seem to…

Show Dex Pratt trying to reach something and hold on to it. Show how the thing is a fish. Show how it's slippery. Show how it's really a bird. Show how it flies away. Show how it's actually a joint as big as his thumb and show how he is choking to death. And then don't show that at all.

chapter 26
september 29, this year.

Getting through the cluster of reporters, even at 8:00 AM is like swimming upstream. I've answered the same questions so many times, my voice is hoarse. When I talk, I can taste sandpaper, the wood dust of a thousand lies. My tongue is dry again, still, always. I've forgotten what is true. A lot of the "reporters" look like kids from my school who I can't quite place. They are strange, misshapen reporters. They aren't real, glossy TV reporters. They are from the free newspapers you get in the box on the corner. They are pretend reporters. We are all pretend. They are making it up. I am making it up.

Everything is made up.

Guess what I've been doing?

I have been smoking.

And smoking.

And smoking.

I inhale inhale inhale, but the trick is not to exhale, not ever, so that inside you become the smoke and the smoke becomes you. Picture a place where organs used to be and instead, now, there is the cool fog of smoke, a gray emptiness that is a relief.

I have to stop.

There is no way that I can fucking stop.

Not now. It's too late.

I don't think I could take clarity. I need the blur to be able to see anything at all.

Feral and I went to Central America last year. SD had business. Mom loves the sun. The beach had sand that was so fine, you could mistake it for cocaine and snort it. You don't think about the beaches in Central America. Belize. Or do you? I used to think of coffee and cocaine. But now, the beach. The beach was awesome.

Feral and I went diving. The water was a dark turquoise blue, a color that seemed impossible but was real. It was so pretty, it seemed...

Safe.

Another lie. The blues always lie. Think about that: cerulean. The sky.

I flipped off the boat like the instructor said and I knew I was in trouble. The panic started before I was even submerged. I followed Feral. If I could still see him, I was alive and it was okay. And it seemed like it would be a good story to tell later. Diving with a fake license. The way I couldn't concentrate on anything but my breathing sounds in the tubes. And how I breathed so fast I knew I was in trouble, panting like a dog, drowning. I hate water. I hate it. I can't stay away from it, but I hate it. I knew which way was up. We never dove so deep that I lost the sun. But even though I knew which way was up, I always felt like it was wrong. Like down was up. I couldn't get it right. My body just wanted me to swim for the bottom when I needed air. Twice, three times, Feral left me. He swam up and I went down, and when I looked for him, he was gone and I was gasping. And there were fish there with long noses and rows of jagged teeth, staring me down, cold and empty eyes waiting to see if I was going to be…

Food.

Later he was joking around, like it was funny that I couldn't find my way out. I couldn't find the light.

It was like when Dad threw me into the lake.

It was like the bubbles from my mouth going down instead of up.

It was like forgetting.

All these people.

Like water, always telling goddamn lies about the path to the surface.

I am in a hurry. I have things to do.

Today is the first game of the season. It's kind of lost in all the craziness, but it's important. It's big. It isn't big. It's an exhibition game. Play basketball. That's normal. There are no aliens. Just the ball. A team. A court. Rules. Easy.

It's nothing.

But I can *play*. I don't know what happened in that cornfield, but I do know that my knee is fine. Just fine.

One-hundred-percent fine.

My plan is to look for Coach first thing, explain to him that my knee is better, ask him to put me back in the game. But when I pull open the heavy doors, Olivia is right in front of me, too large, like a giant blocking my path, and I blink hard and she shrinks down again to normal and her hair is so blond, she looks like a model in a catalogue, which, I suddenly remember, is what I was basing her on to begin with, some misdirected mail I was reading in the bathroom.

And then I forget what I was going to do.

"You didn't come," she says. "I thought..." She looks unsure of herself. Her eyes skim off my face and past my shoulder. "I was..." She stops. Then, "Your knee is better, right?"

"Uh," I go. Which, if you think about it, is my standard response to everything these days. "Olivia," I say. "Are you for real?"

"Real?" she says. "What's real?"

"Seriously," I say. "Stop the fucking craziness." A fleck of my spit hits her cheek and she wipes it off. She looks at her hand, surprised, like she'll see something there.

"Dex," she says. "You sound kind of crazy."

"Crop circle craziness!" T-dot whoops. "That's freakin' *insane*! It's off the charts! Man! I tried to *call* you last night but you didn't pick up. Why didn't you call me *back*? *Dude*. Where *were* you? Insanorama!" He's jumping around me while he talks. I want him to stop and just breathe, but I can't figure out the words to say it. His body hits lockers and he doesn't notice, but the percussion clang of it, of him, is so loud. Too loud.

I shrug. "I don't know," I say.

Olivia touches my back and there it is again: how it's cold. "The stone," I say.

"What?" she says.

"There was no stone," I say.

I am getting so confused.

No one can help me.

I looked all over my room for the stone, in the washing machine, everywhere, and I couldn't find it. It was just gone.

"Can we go there *now*?" T-dot shouts. "I gotta see it for real in daylight. Hey, what the fuck is that in your ear? It's freaky."

"What?" I say sharply.

"In your hole, dude," he says. I touch it. It's warm.

"Todd," I say. His real name sounds weird to my ears. "Something weird is..."

"TOTALLY FUCKING AWESOME!" he yells. "This is the best thing ever. I can't believe we pulled it off. I gotta see it, dude."

"We?" I say. I grab his arm. "What did you say?" I am squeezing his arm so tight my knuckles whiten.

"Hey!" he says, surprised. He's not smiling. "That hurts, dude, let go."

I can't let go of his arm. My hand is not my hand. I say, "Tell me what you said."

"Let go of my fucking arm," he says. And just like that, swift and unbelievably hard, he punches me in the stomach. I go down fast, suffocating. I can't breathe.

"Breathe slowly," he says. "Why wouldn't you let go of my arm? Fuck, Dex. That hurt, man."

"Yeah," I say. "I don't know. Sorry." My breath is coming easier. I somehow stand up. He's looking at his arm where you can see red imprints of my fingers.

"What the fuck?" he says again.

"After school," I tell him. "It can wait until after school. Come on, man. It's not going anywhere."

"I can't believe we pulled it off," he whispers.

"Don't say that," I tell him. "Why are you saying that?"

"Figure it out," he says. He shakes his head, like he's shocked or disgusted. Both. "Figure it out for yourself."

I can't stand this feeling. Something bubbles in my chest. It's black water. It's liquid in a syringe. My veins are ice. I rub my eyes.

"See you later!" Olivia says. "Can't wait for the game!"

T-dot doesn't answer her. Instead, he looks at me and says, "Dex."

"What?" I say.

"Dex," he says. "I totally forgot about your knee, man. Is it better? When did *that* happen?"

"Uh," I say.

Olivia is pressing the small of my back, through the small of my back, I look down, like her hand is going to come through my abs. "I gotta go," I tell him.

I let her steer me. But I don't know where we're going. She pushes and I keep walking, and next thing I know we're in the basement. This is where we keep the sports equipment. There is a bin of basketballs the size of a car. I reach out and touch one. Basketballs are real.

Olivia is not.

"I don't want you to freak out," she says. She isn't looking right at me, but somewhere over my head.

"I'm freaked out anyway," I say.

She pushes her glasses up her nose. My glasses. Her nose. The nose I made up.

"We're leaving," she says. "We never meant to stay this long."

"What?" I say. "What?"

"I just...," she says. "Well, you know, we never talk. I thought we might be friends. Same glasses and...you know. So now I need to say goodbye to you, but we're not even friends. I don't know what we are."

"I don't know what *you* are," I say, and it hangs there between us like all the smoke I've been holding. For a minute, I lose her in a fog.

She clears her throat again and again.

"Cough," I say.

She says, "You wanted me to..."

"I didn't want anything," I say. "I'm not such a good friend. You aren't missing much."

She sneezes. Three times in a row. "Allergies." She sighs.

She leans into me. Just for a second. Leans against me. I can feel the weight of her against my chest, lower, my abdomen. It's like she's lying on top of me, but we're standing up. And then she's gone.

I stand there for ages. Far away, I hear the bell go, but I just stand there. Finally, I pick up a ball and spin it on my finger. I do that for ages. Stand there, spinning the ball and watching it. My fingertip burns.

I put the ball down and go upstairs. I have to find Coach and let him know that I'm okay to play.

Outside the front door of the school, there are two or three reporters and a few of those guys who have websites, crazy goddamn guys who think it's all got meaning. Outside the front door. No, they are inside the front door. They are in front of me. A bald, older man grabs my arm and says, "Did you do it? How did you do it?"

I look to the exit, and then Mr. V is there, shooing them away.

"We're running a school here," I hear him say angrily.

My head is starting to ache badly, and there is a burning in the pit of my stomach where T-dot's fist landed. Kids are milling around in the hallway. A lot of them are wearing Our Joe's T-shirts, but not inside out like I am. I don't know why I am wearing it inside out. I am wearing it inside out on purpose. The T-shirts say *LIVE* on the back, in something that looks like it was written by an old typewriter.

On the front is a picture of the crop circle that looks exactly how it looks from my bedroom window.

Where did that picture come from? Was Our Joe in my room? When did he do this? I look closer at the chest of the girl in front of me, and she whacks me in the side of the head. It's not a photo. It's a drawing.

Perfectly proportioned.

"I've got to go," I say out loud. "I've got to go." I grab my backpack and fly out through the door and start running, pushing through the people, ignoring the questions.

I can hear T-dot screaming, "Wait up!" But I don't wait. I run. I run home on my smooth-oiled limbs, my perfect knee. I run through fields. I run so hard that all I can hear is my pulse and the rasp of my breath, and all I can smell is sweat and the faint tang of pot that is always with me.

And always coming from our house.

Our house that is surrounded by reporters.

And cops.

I run harder.

chapter 27

I stagger up the drive. The ground is uneven, and my vision is blurred from sweat dripping in my eyes and stinging. Dad's sitting on the porch in his wheelchair, staring at all the people who are trampling the corn. From here, they look like ants in an ant farm. Big destructive ants. Already the perfect curve of the outside of the knot is flattened on one side. There are vans parked everywhere. Our Joe is charging the reporters and gawkers fifty dollars a day to park on the field. There's a kid in some kind of uniform down there showing people which spot is theirs. Joe'll be able to build a bigger house. A waterslide. A spa. Redemption.

Except he won't.

Tanis is in my head. Tanis is in me. Crooked in my heart. She says, "Our Joe will get what's coming to him."

Which is what?

"I guess you better give me a hand with the shower," Dad goes. "Bad enough that I'm 'elderly,' I don't need to stink too." He nods at a pile of newspapers on the floor. I pick up the top one and skim it. I read: *Elderly renter, Tom Pratt, and his son Dex...*

Dad is older than a lot of other parents around here. This is the kind of town where you have your kids when you're eighteen because there isn't anything else to do. Dad was forty-three when I was born. He had another wife before Mom. He had a whole other family.

I've left that part out on purpose.

Dad has two other sons. He hasn't spoken to them in twenty years. I wonder just how much of a lousy father you have to be before your kids don't talk to you for twenty years.

He is a shitty father.

But he's still my dad. He's just an old man in a wheelchair. Life 1: Dad 0.

I can't hate him, and believe me, I've tried.

"I'll shower you," I go. "No problem." I shed my hoodie and shoes and grab hold of his chair. I release the brake and push him inside, then down the hall to the bathroom. Then I go back and lock the front door. We never lock our door, so the lock itself is almost impossible to turn.

We never have before now, that is.

"This is shit," Dad says. "Bullshit. Wonder how he did it."

"He who?" I say.

"Our Joe," he says.

"Maybe he didn't," I say. "Don't you think maybe...?"

Dad laughs. "Yeah, right. This is real life, Dex. Not a movie."

"Right," I say. My brain storms, the electricity dripping down my back and jolting me upright.

I turn on the taps and the water blasts out too hot, so I wait because that's all I can do. Eventually it regulates, sort of. Almost. And then I strip off and help Dad with his clothes. "This is Gary's job," I want to say. But I don't. He's my goddamn dad.

I step into the steam and half-carry him with me to his shower seat and strap him in. He washes himself, I just stand there, waiting for him to need me again. The water is too hot. It's scalding. He doesn't complain. I can't help but see that his body hair is gray. The skin on his abdomen hangs like an old man's. There is more loose skin on his arm that moves like a sleeve, like he's wearing someone else's body and it's slightly too big. I shudder. Look away. The hot water feels good on my skin. I'm cold and can't seem to get warm. This is as close as I've been in days. The shower drowns out all the noise.

There's a lot of noise.

We finish up and I find him some clean clothes, which he struggles into while I pretend not to watch, standing by in case he falls. It happens sometimes. On top of being partially paralyzed, he has an inner-ear injury that makes him off-balance. I try to avert my eyes while still watching. Out the back window, there is no evidence of the chaos out front. It looks like it always looks.

I breathe in and out. I try not to think about the air and how it tasted and smelled. How real it was.

It was real.

"Dad," I start.

But he interrupts me. "And here we go," he says. "Cops."

I follow his gaze out the window. Coming through the swathe of blackberries and other shrubbery that marks the end of Our Joe's property is the RCMP.

"I won't let them in, Dad," I say. "Don't worry."

"Just get me back into my chair," he says. "I'll deal with it. Shut your mouth."

"Fine," I go. "Fine." I hoist him off the edge of his bed and shove him into the chair hard enough that if he could feel his legs, it probably would have hurt. But he can't feel them, so who cares, right?

"Hey," he says, a warning in his voice.

"What?" I go.

"Careful," he says. His words are sharp and clear. Something is different.

"Did you take your pills?" I say.

"None of your business," he says. "Now get out of my way, I'll take care of this. I knew it was coming. I'm not as dumb as I look."

The knock on the door is loud. I sit down on Dad's unmade bed. Sometimes I hate him. I want him to pay. I want him to pay. I wanted him to pay. And I said, "I don't care what happens to me, but he can pay." I said that. It was a hot day. The ground was cracked and dry. The lake had shrunk back into itself so it was more of a pond, but we still swam in it. For someone who hates water, I sure spend a lot of time in it.

I hate my dad.

I don't hate my dad.

What did I do?

There are cops.

I stand up and start stripping off the sheets. My arms and legs move mechanically, Transformer smooth. I put on the new sheets, pulling each one tight. I can hear men's voices in the front hall, but I can't make out what they are saying.

Then I hear my dad, loud and clear, "Do I need a lawyer for this? You say the word, and I'll call my guy. I don't like where this is going."

"We have to talk to him, sir," a voice says. Then my name is called, loudly. "Dexter Pratt," says the voice. "Don't make us come in and get you."

I finish tucking in the last sheet and I make a decision, because I don't hate my dad but I do hate myself. I'll take the heat. Man up. That's what Dad used to always say when I cried as a kid, a goddamn kid who fell off my bike and bled from my knees and elbows, road burn on my legs. Man up, goddamn it.

But I can't.

What Our Joe did was unforgiveable, and he will pay. Suddenly, I have clarity. Too much clarity. Like the house itself is humming a perfect high C and all around me the glass shatters, and behind all the glass, I see it. Our Joe has to pay for Tanis, but when I compared my dad and Our Joe, at the lake, looking at the cracked ground, I said, "Dad's just as bad, and the whole fucking house is full of..."

And I said, "Foster care would be better."

And I said, "Fuck him and fuck him and fuck Our Joe and fuck you."

What I meant was, "Sorry."

But it came out wrong. How do I explain? I want to explain. I have to explain. I smooth the sheet again and again and pull it tighter, and then I rip it off and lift it again, and it billows up and flattens, and in that second I forget why I hated my dad so much anyway.

I look at myself in the mirror, like I'm checking with myself to see if it's okay. I look like I haven't slept in a week.

Self-consciously, I pat my tufty hair into some semblance of order and square my shoulders. I take a deep breath and step into the front hall.

I am not me, I remind myself. I am just some kid playing me on TV.

This is not real.

chapter 28

My dad is barring the door with his chair, but I can see four RCMP officers in full uniform, guns hanging off their hips. I recognize only one of them. He's the local guy, the guy who's stuck with our little patch of land as his home base. I nod at him and he smiles, like this is a party and not a shitstorm that's about to ruin my life.

"Dex?" he says. I know his kid. Lundstrom. He's on the team.

"Yeah," I go. I make eye contact with Dad.

"Don't say anything," Dad says.

"Look, sir," says Lundstrom, "there's no problem here. We're just asking questions."

"I'm a lawyer," my dad says.

"Can you please step outside, Dex?" says the older-looking guy in this superconversational tone, like we're old friends.

“I don’t know,” I say.

“It’s okay,” says Dad. “Outside.” He gives me a meaningful look. I get it. He wants to keep them out of the house, away from the low-level hum of the grow lights that I don’t even notice anymore but, for anyone else who happens to be listening, is a dead giveaway. And then there’s the smell. Maybe, I think hopefully, maybe they’re not here about the pot at all.

We had a plan. But not all plans are good. I was so high. It was supposed to be like dominoes, falling in a pattern that made the crop circle that symbolized something. But what the fuck, right? And then they would fall and neatly take down Our Joe and Dad, and then there would only be Tan and me and a bunch of stillness. I don’t know what she meant by that or what I was thinking, but she was crying too much to really make any sense.

I go outside and march purposefully down the steps. They follow me closely, like maybe I’m about to make a run for it. I think about it for maybe a second. I have this idea of running through the corn, past the crop knot, beyond and into the corn maze. I imagine them shouting my name. I see myself dodging and running, away from a spray of bullets that come toward me in slow motion, ripping through my skin and bones and showing everyone that underneath it all, I’m just like everyone.

Normal.

A body.

Dark red blood pooling out onto the ground as I reach for it.

Sticky and hot.

Landing.

Dying.

A close-up of my eyes, the light going out. Which happens, you know. I've seen it: the light, dying.

But this isn't a movie.

Nothing is a movie.

My camera is somewhere under the stairs. I wanted to dump it at the airport, but I didn't. I lied. I had an idea that I would dump it at the airport. I could see myself doing it. I saw myself doing it. I filmed myself doing it.

I didn't film myself doing it.

For a while, I believed that I had done it. But I didn't.

There is more to that story.

All lies have background. If you think about it, the truth is like a blank wall, painted white. A lie is paneling, and behind the paneling is a door and behind the door is a tunnel and behind the tunnel is a reason. And isn't that just more interesting, after all?

I want my camera.

I want to run.

About twenty feet from the front door, there's a stone bench. I sit down on it and look up at the policemen who have followed me. The stone is cold through my pants, the kind of cold that makes me think of death and corpses. They don't say anything, but they are staring like they can uncover the truth by just looking for it long enough.

I won't win a staring contest, so I say, "So?"

Lundstrom plops down next to me. I smell toothpaste and sweat. I wonder if they drew straws to see who would be the one to talk to me. He says, "I got it, guys." The other three disperse into the overgrown roses that mark the front "lawn" of our house. There are some still blooming, big fat red flowers that look like red balloons bobbing against the pale gray sky.

There are bees, even though it should be too cold for them by now. One lands on Lundstrom's leg. "Shit," he says and flicks it off. Then catching my look, he says, "Sorry, I'm allergic."

"Global warming," I say.

"What?" he asks.

"It's not cold enough for them to die," I say.

"Oh," he says. He looks tired. He looks like someone's dad. He *is* someone's dad.

He straightens up and flips open his little notebook. I always wonder why cops have such tiny little pads of paper. This guy looks like he can hardly see it, it's so small. He holds it at arm's length and squints. Wouldn't it be easier to write on a clipboard? A laptop?

In the distance, there's a rainbow. It looks surreal over the backdrop of Our Joe's usually quiet farm, now alive with all the freaks who travel far and wide to see crop circles to prove the point of their own existence. It's like all the grubs in the dirt have become overgrown and are giants, swarming the land. I've seen license plates from as far away as Georgia and New Brunswick.

Come on. It's just a crop circle. Don't these things pop up every day?

I don't realize that I say it out loud until he goes, "I've never seen anything like it. And before this, I worked on the prairies. Nothing but corn and wheat as far as the eye could see."

We sit there side by side, just watching. Because this part of our yard is higher than the fields, we can see everything.

Then he suddenly shakes, like he's snapping himself awake or a ghost is on his grave and says, "Right, okay. We are following up on reports that you are"—he flips open his notebook to a different page and squints at his own handwriting—"'bragging all over school' about how you 'engineered and built the design yourself using a piece of lumber and a...'" He pauses. "And a...horse?"

"A horse?" I repeat. I don't even know how to respond. I swallow a laugh. How could a horse and piece of lumber make a design this big? I look at him. He's not laughing.

"Um," I say. "Well, that's ridiculous. I don't have a horse. I mean, the only horses in town are Zach's. I've never even ridden one. A horse. I wouldn't know how."

"We have a signed statement from a witness who says she—" He coughs. "Excuse me," he says. "Who says she or he saw you with dirt on your clothes and you looked like you'd been…exerting."

"I was running," I say. "Look. A piece of wood and a horse? That would be impossible. *Look* at that thing."

He scratches his head with his pen and sighs. "We have to follow up," he says. "Did you do it?"

"Can you even ask me that?" I say.

"You can tell me whatever you want to tell me," he says.

"Right," I go. "But that's entrapment, right?"

He gives me a long, hard stare. "Kid," he says, "you watch too much TV."

"I think my dad should be here," I say.

"Fine, get him," he says. He looks like a stone wall, his jaw is set so tight.

"I will," I say.

I stand up on shaking legs and go up to the porch where my dad is sitting, smoking. A regular cigarette, of course. Nothing illegal.

"Dad," I go.

At first I think he's mad; then he breaks into laughter. "They think you did it, eh?" he says. "That's the funniest thing I've ever heard. I thought they were here about... well, the other *thing*."

He wheels down the ramp so quick that his chair bounces on the uneven ground. I think he's going to tip over and fall out, but he recovers. I watch, without helping, as he approaches Lundstrom. I can't hear what they are saying. My ears are ringing. All of a sudden, I'm back in the field. Dirt on my back. The light. The smell. The smooth marble slick of the giant eyes.

I fall back into the chair and scream, but it comes out as more of a gasp. Sweat is pouring down my brow.

"You okay, Dex?" It's Dad, wheeling slowly back up the ramp. The RCMP are gone.

I nod. "Panic attack," I whisper. I'm so dizzy.

He looks at me quizzically.

"They're gone," he says finally. "But they'll be back."

At first, I think he's talking about the *aliens*. Because if I did make this crop circle, then the aliens weren't real. But they were. They goddamn were. And I didn't make this crop circle because I still don't know how but I do remember something about a tractor and some boards and a map and I don't want to know.

"I don't want to know," I say.

"They wouldn't charge you with much more than mischief anyway," he says. "Not much of a crime to draw a picture in a field."

"Get it together," I mutter.

"What?" he says.

"I mean, yeah," I say. "Okay. Whatever."

"We're going to have to do something," he says, shaking his head. "What a goddamned mess."

I can hear him rolling away, but I can't stand up and follow him. My legs are shaking too hard. It's probably five o'clock already.

I've missed the game.

This is part of the plan. This is the first part. But I can't remember the second part and I'm so hungry. I can't feel my hands.

I put my head down and I cry hard and suddenly, like a summer squall. Just for a few minutes. Not long enough that anyone sees me—at least I don't think that they do.

chapter 29
september 30, this year.

I am up early enough to cook, so I do. I am in the kitchen making an omelet. Omelets are my specialty. I probably haven't mentioned that.

I slice the garlic as thin as paper, and it turns sweet in the pool of melted butter in the hot pan. I am very precise when I cook. With everything else, I'm a slob. Ask anyone. My writing is awful. I never do my work. The house is a mess, most of the time. The toilets are disgusting.

I add some tiny tomatoes, so miniature they are the size of peas. They steam open and burst. I stir in the eggs. Salt and pepper.

Gary wanders in and sniffs the air. "Smells good," he says. I grunt. I guess I have to feed him too, but I resent it. It's all I can do not to spit in the pan.

"Gary," I say. "Gary, I've been wondering about...your processing. You know? I've been..."

He gives me his patented Gary look. The one that says, "Shut the fuck up."

"It's not for you to smoke, you little prick," he says. But he says it so casually, it takes me a minute to register his words. He leans so close that I can smell a mint on his breath. "It's for the *clients*." He grins. "Paying clients. Should I charge you? How much do you think you owe me?" One of his teeth is entirely gold.

The omelet cooks up fluffy and perfect. I flip it in the air and it lands in the pan with a satisfying plop. "Nothing," I say, quietly so he can't hear me.

I plate it and put the egg in front of dad. He's at his usual place at the table, just looking at the new yellow house. Not moving. Not touching anything. He's too still. Something is going on.

"What's on your mind?" I say. "Dad?"

"I'm tired," he says abruptly. "Don't know how much of this I can eat."

I shrug like I don't care, but the truth is that I do. I want him to eat it. I want him to fucking *love* it. I want a lot of things. That's how this all started. And why.

We'd take the money, me and Tanis. And go. To New York. Somewhere. There's enough money. She'd go with me. All along she's been the kind of girl who wants to leave.

Mexico. That's the other part of the plan. The part. I don't.

I do.

I did.

"Dad," I say quietly. "I saw something in the field that day that wasn't...I can't explain." Even as I'm saying it, it tastes like a lie, bitter and blue.

He nods. Squints at me. "Were you smoking?"

I nod.

"Well," he says, "maybe it just didn't seem real. Could have been a machine or something."

"A machine?" I say. "What kind of machine makes *that*?" I jerk my head toward the window so vehemently that it feels like I pull a muscle in my neck.

"I don't know," he says. "Our Joe is...well, he's making a bunch of money, isn't he? He has something to do with it. Those T-shirts were printed up before the thing even happened, right? They had to have been. That's what I'm thinking."

And then there is Tanis again, her voice, in my head, in my head, in my head, saying, "I'll have the T-shirts printed up, and it will look like he..."

"Dad," I say, "Our Joe is too..." I stop. I think. I think about me and Tanis on a bus or a goddamn plane or something, and New York is a big city. I close my eyes and think about an apartment. Cockroaches. The sounds of a city that never is so quiet that you have to hear yourself think. How would we cross the border though? We are underage and there are laws. Why didn't we think of that?

"I don't know if Our Joe...," I start again. Then I say, "The T-shirts make him seem pretty guilty, huh? But who cares anyway? It's not like he's...killing someone. He won't even go to jail. Or...But..."

"He could," says Dad. "Mischief, maybe."

It feels like a thousand years since I was lying out there, being dwarfed by all that sky and all that pot and feeling like my problems were the biggest in the world. Now, suddenly, everything feels impossible. Everything is impossible. Our plan is so stupid and full of holes and sinking in the middle of a turquoise ocean in the fog, the thick fog. What was I thinking?

"I'm going to go out," I say. "I think there's somewhere I have to go." I am almost remembering. I am close to remembering all the pieces of the puzzle; I think I remember. I close my eyes and there it is again: the tightly packed gray-brown earth that we called the "beach"; the trees with the tiny green leaves that didn't give enough shade; and the way the water had pulled away so the raft was only a few feet from the shore. And the sun. It was so hot. I am remembering like it's a film, but the soundtrack isn't on and it's a silent movie and I'm in it and I can see myself, my mouth moving and Tanis leaning into me and saying, “Yes.” Nodding. “Yes.” Her pink lips saying, “Yes.” And New York tasting so brave.

“Live,” said Kate. “So we do this thing, right? We do this thing and then he pays and you get your life back? Like that? And maybe we double it up, right? And Dex gets his back too.”

I remember nodding. “Yeah,” I said. “Fuck them all.”

I remember Tanis saying something, like, “It’s different, but whatever.”

I remember T-dot saying, “I don’t know, man, but it’s up to you guys, it’s your thing. We’re just helping. But, you know, it could go wrong anywhere along the line.”

I remember. I don’t remember.

I am making this up. It’s a story. I am telling myself a story. I don’t remember anything. I am making something fit that doesn’t fit. A sweater that isn’t mine. This town. My life. Tanis.

I am sweating. It’s dripping off my nose like I’ve been running. I have been running. I am tired of running. I want to live in a split-level in the suburbs. I want my dad to grow *tomatoes*. I want Our Joe to pay for something, even if I don’t want to know what it is. I want everyone to pay, I want Gary to pay, I want my dad to pay and everyone, and maybe this was my idea.

I am going to be sick.

Was it my idea?

I don't have ideas.

I have movies that play out in my head. It's a movie. It's just a movie and none of this matters or is real or will matter in a hundred years or...

It's a low-budget movie. A romance, an adventure, something old-fashioned where, at the end, the hero and his girl get out of town. And the other stuff is slow motion and implied. And then they are in New York, the jumble of it, implying happily ever after, implying everything.

"Happily ever after," I say out loud to myself, to no one, and out of my mouth the smoke keeps coming and coming and coming.

I am close to knowing something I don't want to know. And there is smoke in my eyes, the smoke alarm going off, my eyes burning, the smell of pot everywhere. I can't breathe in this room, and I go to open the screen door and...

"Where are you going?" Dad says. "You're pretty late for school, aren't you? Don't get abducted on your way."

"Hilarious," I say. "Funny, Dad. You need anything before I go?"

"Nah," he says, then adds, "Gary's here."

I head out the door. I'm not going to school. School seems like something I've never done. Why do I need school? I turn north and just walk. I scratch my legs raw on the blackberries, just plunging through them like I don't care, because I don't. I like it. The scratching of my skin, the way my skin so easily opens and bleeds, crisscrossed with bloody x's. The foothills are low and rocky. I walk with no plan. I walk. I just keep going. I start to climb.

I walk and climb until I get to the wall of the valley. Our valley. It's sheer and slippery, but I avoid the road, the easy path. I need to do something hard. Something impossible. I need to hurt. I need to fucking crawl in gravel and *feel* it.

I need to feel it.

I start to climb for real. The rock is as cold as the stone bench outside our house and as smooth as ice. It stops me from having to think about much else. All there is is me and the rock, and my hands, bleeding and raw, just barely holding me up, and the sound of my heavy breathing and grunting from the effort and the wind, just enough you can hear it, and birds. There are always birds.

About halfway up there's a ledge, and I haul myself up on it, gasping.

I sit there for a long time. I have a bottle of water in my pocket and I drink it. It tastes like stale plastic. I can't get enough of it all the same. I flip open my phone and scroll through my contacts. I could call Feral. I could call Mom. I could call anyone. Look at all these people who I never call. Phil Stars? Give me a fucking break. Like I'll ever call him to just shoot the shit. As if.

I call Tanis. It takes her ages to pick up.

"Dex," she says.

"Tanis," I say. "I don't know. I just think New York might never have worked anyway."

"What?" she asks. "What are you talking about, Dex?"

"I don't know," I say. "I just...I don't feel well."

"Are you okay?" she asks. "Why aren't you here? Mrs. D is pissed."

"Tell her I'm researching my paper," I say. I hear paper rustling.

"I've got to go, Dex," she says. "I'll call you later, okay? Don't freak out, Dex. We're so close."

"Okay," I say. "Tanis?"

She doesn't answer. I don't know if she's still there or not. "Tan?" I say. "I love you."

I hang up.

Tanis is real, I remind myself.

I want to call her back. I want to say, "Not my dad." Or "No." Or something so she knows I've changed my mind. I can't.

But it's probably too late.

Glass came to town last March. I wasn't expecting her. Ever. Having Glass in this town was nothing but totally impossible. She roared into town in her Mercedes, and everyone stared. It was like the whole place shrank as she approached it.

I was in Wing's, or the shithole that everyone calls Wing's even though it's been called the Purple Garden for years. Tanis and I were holding hands, but when Glass screeched to a stop outside, I dropped Tanis's hands like they were something disgusting, like a cockroach in the noodles, and I couldn't get far enough away from them. I watched through the window as Glass adjusted her hair and lip gloss and gave a little bounce as she got out of the car. Somehow she saw me through the window and came tearing in.

"DEX, you fucking HOT STUD!" she screamed.

Tanis got up and left. Just like that.

Glass hadn't called me in months by then. I moved in winter. It was spring. There was some kind of goddamn blossom tree opening up in the parking lot, and the flowers made the whole place look nicer than it ever really was. I'd forgotten the exact shade of her purple hair, the way she waved her hand in front of her all the time like she was wiping away cobwebs when she talked. The way her tongue crept out of her mouth when she paused for the next word and tapped her top lip. That used to make me crazy.

"What are you doing here?" I said. I couldn't decide if I was happy or sad or just pissed off. And I wanted to know where Tanis was. I was always looking after girls who were walking away, and there was always another one standing in front of me.

Then I saw, in Glass's car, someone else.

Feral.

Frank.

I walked out of the restaurant and he was just sitting there. Sunglasses on the back of his head like a douche bag. It was cloudy but bright. He looked smaller. He probably was. More cheekbones, less cheek. He smiled but it didn't make it up as far as his eyes or really anywhere past his mouth.

He looked like shit.

He looked like an addict.

He looked high.

I was so pissed with him. For wrecking it. For taking the whole glam-boy prep-school drug-dabbler rock-band BULLSHIT and turning it from something that was a fucking lark into a serious death wish and a head that was one step away from skeletal.

"Douche bag," I said. It was the backward glasses and the way they pissed me off.

I could see even by the way he moved his arms, the way he took the glasses carefully off the back of his head, put them on his face, then tipped them down so he could look at me over the top, eyes as dilated as marbles. "Bro," he said.

I didn't do any of what I wanted to do:

Punch him.

Cry.

Scream.

I just walked away.

I wanted heroin.

I wanted Feral to die.

I wanted to die.

I wanted I wanted I wanted.

The bubbling in the needle. The exhalation of relief when you find the surface is closer than you think.

I cried.

I was walking. Side of the highway. Not running. Not fast. Just walking. Trying, but also not trying, to get away. Glass slowed the car down beside me. I hated her. I hated her car.

"Hey," said Feral. "Brought you this."

He dumped it on the side of the road. It probably broke. I didn't check. Just picked it up and kept walking. My feet slapping the pavement, one step two three four five. I was counting and I kept counting, holding my camera in my arms like a baby and I walked all the way home the long way, along real roads, and beside me was corn. Miles of corn.

That much corn can make you feel crazy. Rustling. Like it's telling you things that aren't possible but they are. Whispering stories that you start to believe.

Feral died in August, right before school went back. Right before we made the Plan. LIVE. Fucking LIVE.

Which is why, maybe, I wasn't paying enough attention to anything except trying to smoke enough that the water would close over me and fill up my ears so that I didn't have to hear Dad saying, "Dex. Dex. You can go if you want to, Dex. Not that I ever saw the point in funerals in the first place."

Water does a good job of filling in just enough space that the rest of the sounds are blocked out. The ringing phones. The way Dad kept saying, "Dex." The way Tanis said, "Talk to me, Dex." The way T-dot, said, "Man, Dex." The way everyone was saying "Dex Dex Dex Dex Dex" until I didn't want to hear my own name at all. And I didn't want to hear Feral's either. So I swam deeper.

Let's just say that. I went as deep as I could go.

I left that part out on purpose before because it didn't matter because he was dead. But it did matter. It always matters when someone dies even if you say, "He was already dead to me anyway and he *was* already dead." But the thing was, he wasn't dead. And then he was. So when he actually died for real, I just thought that I could say, "Fuck the whole world." And somehow it was Dad's fault.

But it wasn't.

It was Feral's. And he was dead, forever dead. The cold rotting corpse in the ground kind of dead...with maggots. And I didn't want that, so I went on thinking about him at St. Joe's in one of those white shirts. And then I smoked some more and made The Plan, and smoked again and pretended that it hadn't happened and nothing was real.

Pretending is like a gentle lie. Pretending is blurring the lens so you don't have to see what you aren't ready to see.

I am refilming the ending. I don't know what it will be, but it won't be that. It won't have anything to do with how I didn't go to my own brother's funeral because I am more of a douche bag than he will ever be, that fucking douche bag. I hate him not even close to how much I hate myself.

I drag myself back to the moment. Be in the moment. That's some kind of Buddhist shit that Tanis talks about and I pretend to understand and take it in. And I don't really understand it or take it in. It sounds a lot like the stuff that my mom used to talk about, finding her "center" and being one with herself, which excused her for the fact that she lied and cheated and then she *left*.

And I don't feel at one with myself or anyone else. And I can't sit and listen to nothing. And the birds are making me think of something I remember that might be a nightmare or real or somewhere in between.

I sit on the flat unrelenting rock and I think and I don't get high. I want to. I have five jays rolled and ready in my pocket. I hold them in my hand and look at them, and who the fuck cares if I smoke them or not? I want to make like someone does, but no one does, so that's bullshit too. I unroll one and crumble the shit between my fingers and then just let it fall to the ground. The smell of it makes me think of something hopeless, like a dried-up caterpillar that died in its cocoon and never became a moth or a butterfly or whatever it thought was going to happen when it crawled in there. Dried caterpillars. That's what it smells like. Hopelessness and the corpse of something that was meant to be something else.

My mouth is so dry. My insides are dry. My throat. I imagine that if you cut me open, I'd be crumbly inside just exactly like a dried plant, and maybe I'm getting mixed up with some kind of kids' story, but maybe *I'm* not real anymore because somewhere along the way someone forgot to love me.

That's the kind of crap that I think about when I have to think and I'm not high. I'd rather be high and thinking about how high-fructose corn syrup is going to wipe out America, than not high and thinking about how I'm not even real.

That's fucked up.

I'm fucked up.

Even though it tastes like shit, all that water makes me feel clean. I drink and drink and drink. I eat an apple and a granola bar and I get a fake feeling of wholesomeness, like an actor on TV who advertises kayak adventures or bungee jumps, but who is really a drug-addled wreck. Someone playing a fresh-milk kind of guy.

I sit and sit. Until I can't even feel my ass, that's how long I sit for. The light changes, like the day itself is letting out a long, slow sigh. The corn looks like a lawn from here. Tiny and inconsequential. The Celtic knot is unrecognizable.

I concentrate on breathing, which freaks me out slightly and makes me feel like I've forgotten how to do even that properly.

My dad is probably worried, but I can't bring myself to move. School must be over by now. It's almost twilight.

Maybe I fall asleep.

I definitely fall asleep.

I don't dream.

There is no movie.

Maybe there are no movies left in me; maybe just like that, they've gone.

And the aliens came down and touched us with their white hands and everything was cured forevermore.

Yeah, right.

I put the camera under the stairs where we were storing all the furniture from the old house that didn't fit in any of the real rooms. The space under the house was huge. Cavernous. Dark.

Which is where that camera belonged.

In the dark.

I went into the dark to put the camera in there, and that's when I found the boxes. Of photographs. The boxes and boxes of photographs. That's the part I don't want to remember. That's it and now I'm remembering it. I'll tell you why I don't want to: it's because, when you see pictures of some people as a kid, you don't recognize them. Because they don't have a genetic defect that gave them a crooked grin. When they were a baby, when they were five or seven or eight or…

All those pictures. Why would he even keep them?

Evidence.

You never want to see pictures like that of anyone, not any kid. There is an evil that does that to kids. An evil that makes petty evils like drugs and pot and your parents' fights seem like a joke. The worst thing.

Which is why Tanis was always hiding in her numbers and how she could never make anything add up to why anyone would do that to her.

Anyone.

"Some things you see, you can never unsee." That's from a Nicholas Cage movie called *8MM*. And it's true. I can't unsee. I can't not make Our Joe pay.

But if.

I could have hidden the camera anywhere. I could never have opened those boxes. I could just have turned him in, but then it turned into this sideshow. Somehow. It was symbolic, she said.

I would have done anything for her because I knew and I had to save her, even though I had thought that it was her job to save me. Do you see?

I see.

I don't want to see.

It was so grandiose. A crop circle. The T-shirts. It got more and more layered and I got lost. But when and where and where and when did the aliens come into it?

Because we can't have done that.

So it wasn't real.

It was.

It's the one piece that doesn't fit. Two pieces: Olivia.

Now that I remember, I don't want to remember. Can I unremember?

I could jump. From here. This cliff. I could just quit this fucking plan. I don't want my dad to pay for a big, romantic, movie-worthy gesture, because I just realized that the movie doesn't quite make sense. And if it was a script, we'd need to fix the ending because why didn't I just call the cops right then and *tell*?

Because.

Because I wanted my dad to pay too.

Because I am tiny. So tiny he can barely even see me anymore, not even through his bifocals.

The field looks quiet tonight. From here, the crop circle is lit by the glow of floodlights.

I think that none of this matters. Nothing matters.

I flip open my phone. I want to call Olivia, but I don't know her number. I want to call her, but what would I say? "Hi, it's me"?

You can't call someone who doesn't exist.

There are the stars, same as the other night. There's the ground holding me up. There's me, lying down. I can feel myself starting to relax. I have to be careful though, because if I get too high, I won't be able to climb back down. I won't want to bother. I don't remember the moment when I swept the pot back up and rolled it into a joint with all the rest of what I had, five joints in one, it looks like a goddamn cigar. And there it is, in my hand.

What about the milk? I think.

Then I pull all that smoke in and hold it tight, lungs clenched white-knuckled tight, starbursts falling in front of my eyes, my highs, my...

I have music in my head. Songs we played or never got around to playing or practiced or said we were going to practice. It's all mixed up, jumbled up, messed up, fucked up.

Like me.

chapter 30

FLASHBACK TO:

INT.—STORAGE UNIT WHERE BAND EQUIPMENT IS SET UP

Show the band, practicing. Feral. Me. A guy named Jon. His twin sister Reid. Show the instruments. Zoom in close on our hands.

Show Dex Pratt playing the bass guitar. He's pretty good. Show his fingers. Close up on the fingers. Closer and closer until what you actually see is the whorls of his fingerprints and turn that into a Celtic knot into a crop circle and pan out. And now you're really losing it, Dex Pratt.

Cut that entire scene and put the fucking camera in the trash at an airport.

Start again.

Show the band, warming up. Discordant chords. Show that it's dark outside. Show kids outside, waiting to listen. Show the band drinking. Show the mark on Dex Pratt's arm. Show him stabbing the needle in. Show him giving the needle to Feral. Show Feral shaking his head.

Show Feral running.

Show the band playing without him.

Show Feral coming back, picking up the guitar. Show him putting down the guitar. Show him punching the living shit out of Dex. Show Dex's half-smile. Show him slumping down to the floor. Show that.

Show it again.

Put it in a loop and show it over and over again.

Zoom in on that tattoo inside his elbow and zoom out and make that the Celtic knot and the crop circle...

And...

CUT.

Wait.

Dex Pratt is on a ledge. In the valley. Above the valley.

He is baked. Show how he is baked. Zoom the camera in on his eyes. His pupils are huge. Which actually is weird because usually when he smokes pot, his pupils shrink. Discuss the difference. Don't discuss anything.

Zoom in to the black of his pupils and then zoom out and they are not his pupils, they are the black moving surfaces of the eyes of a...

No, don't do that.

It isn't that kind of movie.

Use the black surface to show the reflection of the guy holding the camera, and the guy is Dex, and zoom in on his eye and show in the reflection that it's also Dex. Dex and Dex and Dex, and he exists in so many layers, but in each of them he is alone.

Show Dex on the ledge. Make the soundtrack something haunting or else some kind of song that's a tearjerker. Ideally, Coldplay's "Fix You." That will get the audience rooting for Dex somehow being fixed.

Show how Dex is unfixable.

Show...

DEX

Holy shit, not this again.

Show some kind of blinding light and then Dex rising up and twirling around. Somehow do that so it doesn't sound as cheesy as it sounds and make it as terrifying as it actually is.

I can't do this now.

CUT.

CUT.

I really fucking mean it.

CUT.

chapter 31

I can't make this stop.

If this isn't real, I can't see how it isn't. I am trying to force my eyes to stay open. It's dizzying—I'm twirling around in the air. My arms and legs are so loose, they keep whipping around and it's like I'm hitting myself. I force myself to not pass out. I force myself to keep breathing, even though the light does not feel like air. And when I look, it appears that the white light is going in through my mouth like smoke. It is going into me and I can't stop it.

I'm really genuinely piss-my-pants scared and I want to get off this fucking ride. Now. I can't even pretend this is a movie that I'm making, because it isn't and I'm not. And the camera is somewhere under Chelsea's old desk under the stairs and I haven't touched it.

I'm going to die, I think.

I keep breathing it all in. It stinks and I feel sick, but I make myself not throw up.

"Stop this," I try to say, but it comes out more like I'm gargling, which I guess I am. Gargling the light. And the light is bubbling in the back of my throat where the air is supposed to go and so it can't, and the light is suffocating me and I am going to...

I try counting but I can't get past ten without feeling like letting go, passing out. I try picturing my mom and my sister. And my dad. I try picturing Olivia. I try picturing Tanis.

I picture the lake.

The light is water.

That's all. Just water.

I know how to swim, because my dad taught me.

I say that part out loud, only not.

I am following the bubbles. I kick my legs. I don't want to fall or sink.

My hands are in my pockets. There are stones in my pockets. Dozens of stones. Stones are pouring out of my pockets. Orange ones. They're warm.

I smash to the ground. It hurts, but I'm awake. I'm aware. I force myself to sit up, but it's like gravity is different. I wish I was high. If I was high, I'd wouldn't be so terrified. I'd be able to sort this out.

"Help," I say out loud, just to see if I can talk.

And then…

This is the part where you say, What the goddamn fuck about this is real?

Because…

Olivia is next to me. Her hand on my arm. Her hand.

My Olivia. Who I made up. Her hand. She was never real. Was she?

I never gave her a name before. She was just The Girl. She was no one. She had no name. She was never meant to have a name.

Her hand, broken nails. Wait. Not nails.

Claws. Fucking *claws*. Her hand has turned pale blue. Then lavender. Her nails are not nails. Her nails are stones, and they fall away and under them are the claws of a bird that isn't a bird.

I think I am screaming.

Her eyes are black vacant pools.

"You came," she says, but in a way that suggests what she's saying is dirty. She leans forward and kisses me. I do not want to kiss her back, but then I am kissing her back. I think I lose consciousness. Am I conscious? My whole body is being touched; I cannot pinpoint sensation or feeling.

I look down, like I wouldn't be surprised to find myself naked, and then…

I'm falling...

Again.

And...

I'm in the dirt. I'm in the dirt and I'm naked. I don't know where I am. Where am I?

I lie on the ground. I can taste dirt in my mouth.

I spit. I sit up. I try to get my bearings. I don't like this. I liked it better when it was a movie, even if it was a movie with no camera and no crew and no director and no actor. Because movies are fiction and they are not real.

I have lost. I am lost. I...

Fell.

Or jumped.

I took my clothes off first because I am...

Naked.

Just like he was.

I didn't really; it wasn't me. And why am I in charge anyway?

Olivia.

I am not broken; I can get up and I can run and there I am, running in the corn again and the dirt is soft under my bare feet. And then I am in the corn maze. I'm right in the center, marked by a statue of Our Joe's dead wife, Roxanne. She looks like she is dancing in a ballet, something that old Roxanne likely never did. She looks young, which she wasn't.

I touch the statue, and it is wet and solid under my hand and definitely there. I am definitely here.

"Roxanne," I say, and my voice sounds normal. Like my voice.

Roxanne looks exactly like Tanis. She has the same facial disfigurement. It's genetic. Roxanne is Tanis's grandmother. But you knew that. I knew that.

Roxanne, Tanis says, is the one who found the pictures, and when she did, Our Joe killed her.

Yes, that is what Tanis says.

What Tanis said.

At the lake.

And why Our Joe will pay.

And why I had to make it so big. *Cinematic*.

My fucking idea because I am the director of everything (of nothing) and she must love me or why would she agree? Why would she let me?

A crop circle?

And it was here. In this corn maze. What Our Joe did. Where Tanis tried to run. "But I wasn't there," I say out loud, and I am crying and I couldn't save her and I can't save her now and I don't know what she wants from me and I still don't know how the crop circle can save her.

LIVE.

Tanis was once running naked in this maze crying and she couldn't get out.

I am naked in this maze. But there is a difference. I can get out. I can breathe. I can do this. I have done this maze before. Naked makes no difference. My penis flaps against my leg.

Our Joe hurt her and took pictures, and the pictures are in boxes in the basement of his house, and those boxes are labeled *Christmas 1994*.

And the RCMP will find them in the raid that we have staged that has to do with the crop circle. That has to do with nothing. But it would look good on film if someone was filming it. But no one is filming it. And this is real life. You can't make the plot go the way you need it to go when you make it up in the first place.

Between here and my house, there are a dozen people. Not really reporters anymore; now it's just handfuls of freaks and conspiracy theorists and kids getting high.

I try to think.

I'm shivering.

It's not like I can go back up the cliff and get my clothes.

Why didn't I die anyway? How can someone fall and not only survive but be fine? How far was it?

I make a decision. I start to slowly walk out of the corn maze. I speed up. I start to run. Who cares? There are so many stars up there. Other planets. Other lives. Billions on this one and billions out there. And I'm just one kid, running naked through the corn, hoping like hell not to run into some jackass with a camera.

chapter 32

When I get to the house, I can see someone sitting on the porch. Just an outline, a shadow.

My heart is going to explode inside me like a Roman candle. If you took my pulse right now, you wouldn't be able to count it, that's how fast it is. T-dot's pen on the desk. Tanis's feet tapping. The percussion of the basketball on the court. All inside me. Too loud, too fast, too ragged.

Who is it?

I can't tell.

All I want is to get inside. Somehow it feels like if I'm inside, I'll be okay. I'll tell Dad. I'll do...something.

I gasp accidentally, just hungry for more air, trying to clear my lungs of the salt-acid taste of...whatever the fuck that was. The gasp makes the person jump up.

I recognize the red boots.

"Why are you naked?" Tanis says. "Dex? What's going on?"

"I was in the corn maze," I say. "Tanis."

"DEX!" I hear her shouting. And then I'm being lifted and not by Tanis. By someone big and tattooed.

Gary.

"What is in that fucking pot?" I mumble, and then I'm in bed and I'm asleep but I'm not. I'm dreaming that I'm not asleep dreaming about sleeping.

Tanis is beside me, and then she's gone and there are hushed conversations. And somehow the hushed conversations make me really fall asleep because there is something about that—about people talking quietly so as not to wake you—that makes you feel taken care of and so tired.

That you can finally sleep.

chapter 33
october 1, this year.

I go to school the next day. It is surreal to go to school. How can I go to school?

The building looks smaller. It's shrunk. The kids look more ordinary. Everything that happens here is ordinary. I want to rub "ordinary" all over me and have it catch.

This is my life. My life is ordinary.

Stacey waves at me from the office. Her sweater is fuzzy and pink and hangs off one shoulder, revealing a fat bra strap. Mr. V stands behind her desk, leaning, like it's an effort to stand up. He's leaning on her shoulder, and she looks up at him and smiles and nods.

They are ordinary.

This is an ordinary place where ordinary things happen, and I'm just an ordinary kid and ordinary is one of those words that, when you repeat it, begins to sound like something it isn't.

Then Coach is in front of me.

"You're expected to go to the games, even if you're injured," he says. He is a man who says everything like a question. A question there is no answer for.

"I know," I say. "Sorry." It's simple and I am sorry. I smile at him. For the first time in ages, I feel almost happy.

"Did you have something to do with that crazy crop circle?" he asks. His breath is bad, like coffee and sausage. I reel backward, bang off a locker.

"Coach," I say. "No. NO."

I lie so easily now. It's all I do. Everything is a lie. People want to believe lies. That's why movies work. Bullshit is better than reality. The lies help everyone to believe in something.

"Okay," he says. "Okay, I believe you. But don't let it get in the way of your game, son. The GAME is the THING."

I say, "Coach, I'll be at practice today, I swear. I've been...my dad was sick."

"Yeah," he says. "Okay. Fine. How's your knee?"

"Better," I say.

"Better?" he asks. "Don't bullshit me, kid. Never bullshit a bullshitter." He laughs like he's made the funniest joke of all time.

I try to laugh too, but it comes out wrong, an air bubble, a balloon of something sad.

"Funny," I say, instead of trying the laugh again.

"Yeah, yeah," he says. "Let's see it then."

I roll up my pants and show him. "It feels okay."

He leans over close and puts his hand on my leg. His fingers are warm and I jump.

"Sorry," he says and pulls back. They aren't supposed to touch us.

"You can come to practice," he says. "But the second it starts to hurt, you're out, understood? But you stay. You don't get to slack off. Understand me?"

I nod. I am not dizzy. I am fine. My knee is fine.

I sit down in the foyer. The benches are stomach-acid green vinyl with years of words written in ink. Holes made by a million fingers. They are browning with dirt that will never come off. It's quiet. I can hear the clock tick.

I wait. I watch through the glass for a familiar car, and then, suddenly, there it is. I run outside. The air is cold like it has finally let go of summer and resigned itself to the Octoberness of the now and become autumn.

I grab Olivia's arm hard and pull her like a little kid over to the tree, the big oak tree. The leaves are as red as blood, outlined with migraine-shimmer silver, and I am...

"Stop it," I say.

"What's got into you?" she asks. "Wow."

"Wow?" I say. "You KNOW what it is."

She doesn't look in my eyes. She won't look at me at all. Her eyes are whirling from one thing to another. Never landing, a hopping bird, intent on not being caught.

I'm still hanging on to her arm. Probably my fingers are leaving marks, or would be if there was anything to leave a mark on, my own nails digging into my own palm. Where does the lie begin and end, and why can I still see her?

I drop her arm and she lets it fall, looking at it like it's something that just happened to be in her coat.

"Why are you fucking with me?" I ask. "You aren't real."

There's a long silence. A crow flies from the fence to a branch overhead and starts to call. His beak is open, and he's staring at Olivia. She is a small bird and he is a crow, and she is small enough. The crow stares and calls. She gives a small, low cry.

"Sorry," she says. "Crows freak me out."

"Yeah?" I go. "Well, you know what freaks *me* out? You."

"Really?" she says. Her voice is faint. Scratchy. Like a recording. "You don't like me?"

I want to shake her. I want to hurt her. I ball my hands up by my sides. What is happening to me? I can't kill someone who's not there. I imagine my hands around her throat. My hands on my own throat. I want I want I want.

I don't know what I want. She's what I wanted. I think about Tanis. New York City, right? I want New York. I don't know what I think I'd do in New York. Work in some shitty restaurant? Who would hire me? What would I really *do*?

"I love you," I say. "But you aren't really here." I am crying. My tears are fish and they roll down my cheeks and into a lake that I'm standing in. There is water around my feet. I'm standing in water. What is it with this water?

Olivia opens her blue eyes wide and turns to look at me. I force myself to look back. Her eyes are not blue. They are a color that is not a color. An oil slick on a rain-wet road. A tar pit. A mermaid's call.

"You," I say. I want to run, but I stand my ground. "You aren't real. I made you up." I'm really bawling. The kind of crying you do when you are a kid and your dad tries to kill himself, that kind. The kind that almost kills you and doesn't. The ugly kind with snot bubbles and blinding tears. "I don't want to drown," I say.

"I have to go somewhere," she says. She flickers. She frowns, like she can't think what it is she is meant to be doing. Where she has to go.

I blink. Squint. My eyes are blurry. The tree is draped around us like a curtain.

The tree is draped around *me* like a curtain.

I am alone. I am sitting on the ground, which is cool and damp. An empty chip bag is beside me and the wind moves it and it rustles. I can see the writing on the bag so clearly, it's like all of a sudden I can see. I couldn't see before. I can see. There is nothing between my eyes and the bag. I look at my hand. It looks like my hand. My hand that I can always remember seeing, holding a book in front of my face. A camera in front of my face. A joint in front of my face. My hand that is always holding something in front of my face. It's empty. I turn it over and look at the lines on my palm, clear and precise, like they were drawn there. Turn it over again, and I can see each hair, a pattern of veins. Normal. I have a normal hand.

"Olivia," I say. There are crows in the tree and they call. It sounds like they are saying my name.

The crows are not saying my name.

There is an orange stone in my (normal) hand, and then there are a hundred orange stones spilling out between my fingers. They rain down out of my hand and onto my feet until I'm standing in a puddle of orange pebbles but the pebbles turn into leaves before I can throw them at the birds, which is what I was going to do.

I was going to.

I was...

I lean over and vomit. My vomit soaks into the ground, covers the leaves, spatters the tree. I vomit myself inside out. I vomit until I can't stop.

I don't understand, I think. But then again, also, I do.

I understand enough.

I'm lying.

I don't understand a fucking thing.

I sit down and lean my back against the tree, but the smell of my own puke is too much. A crow swoops down and eyes the puke, digs in.

Through the veil of leaves, I can see T-dot running toward me, so I get up. I wipe my mouth. I take a breath and push aside the branches that are hiding me.

"I got to tell you something, man," T-dot says. "It's important."

I squint. Everything is important.

"Yeah?" I sigh. "What?"

He goes, "Lundstrom's saying that his dad is gonna bust up your place. So it's going to happen. Just like we...I was just thinking, maybe you don't want it to happen? I don't know, man, it doesn't feel right."

"Thanks," I manage to say. "I gotta go."

I am trying to think.

Can I think?

I don't know which way to go. I get in the car. Dad's car. I have the car. I don't remember driving here, but I must have because now I'm in the car and the engine is roaring and I'm driving faster than I should, but now is not the time to slow down. Not yet.

chapter 34

My dad is in the basement. He is on the floor. He has gathered up all the plants, dumped them from their pots. There is a pile of dirt on the floor beside him and empty plastic pots tossed into the corner. The plants are in his arms. How many plants? Ten? Twelve?

Gary is with him. Of course Gary is with him; Gary is always with him. Only Gary isn't helping him; Gary is helping himself to the plants. I want *Gary* to get fucking caught. Not Dad. I am on the stairs, out of breath—my lungs are empty balloons and refuse to fill up. I gasp and gasp. But I am just trying to say what they already know. How did they know?

I thought I was the director. This film didn't end this way. It just didn't. It ended with Dad being caught,

Dad paying the price for his goddamn choices. And me and Tanis in New York City and Our Joe in jail and and and…

Then the credits, rolling.

I forgot about Gary.

Gary is taking what he can, and Dad is grabbing it back, but why?

I see Gary push my dad, and then my voice comes back and I say, "Don't fucking touch him."

"Yeah?" says Gary. "Like you can stop me."

My fists curl up by my sides like I am going to do something, which I don't do, and instead Gary pushes past me roughly and I fall the last three steps to the floor, jarring my knee.

Something pops in my *knee*.

I feel a tearing, deep inside. But this has already happened, I think.

I hear Gary's bike roar to life.

My dad is cradling an armful of plants, and only when I look closely do I see that they are tomatoes, not pot. I think he is laughing or maybe he's crying. I grew those plants.

Because he used to. I don't know why, it just seemed like the right thing to do.

"They are just plants," I say. My breath tastes like stomach acid and eggs.

I help Dad up. Of course he can't stand. His legs buckle. I push him onto Chelsea's old bed in the corner.

"I forgot," he says. "Tomatoes." He looks dazed. "I'm sorry. I ruined your crop."

"Dad," I choke. "Dad."

"Open the back door," he says. "I can't reach. We aren't done here." He puts the tomato plants down on the bed beside him. The bed still has a pink bottom sheet on it. He lays the plants out like they matter. He smoothes the sheet. He looks so pathetic and small. When did he get so small? Maybe he is the tiny one in all of this, maybe when he jumped from that grain elevator, he just got smaller and smaller until he hit the ground.

I forget for a minute that this is my doing, that I wanted him to get caught. And to be taken away and for me to be set free of this.

This.

But this is my home and this is my dad and I don't know what I was thinking and I don't know what I'm thinking now except, No, I don't want this after all.

I go and open the door, and the cold, bright air rushes in on a wave of watery light.

The doorbell rings upstairs. I freeze and my blood runs cold. I think maybe I'm going to pass out again, the floor pounding into my skull.

But Gary didn't take all the plants. There is a whole table behind me of pot plants that are just starting to bud. Rows and rows.

"Fuck the tomatoes," I say. "Do something."

I hear the front door opening. Footsteps on the stairs. I'm frozen. I can't move. My legs don't work. I have a ghost of a memory, so faint I can hardly see it. It's like looking through milk, opaque, impossible. I think I remember a plan. I can see Kate, nodding. I can hear Kate saying, "They'll find the Christmas boxes when they find the pot."

Was it Kate?

An arm draped around my back. The smell of beer and laughter. A drawing. A piece of paper. Tanis's cheeks and how they flushed while she explained.

"Our Joe is going to pay."

"Your dad is going to pay."

I have a taste in my mouth. Bile. Acid.

There are footsteps on the stairs.

My psychiatrist has a name for what I do. He calls it "selective editing." As soon as he gave it a name, I started doing it more and more. Is that how it's supposed to work?

I have been lying. Lying and editing are the same thing. A few edits can change a story into something else. Edit someone in. Edit something out. It's so easy. Stories change as you tell them. You think, "Okay, this is the screenplay that I'm writing." But even as it's being acted out, you're the director. You can still change shit. And so you do. It's never done until it's done.

Tanis comes down the stairs.

"I've changed my mind," I say. "About New York."

"It's too late," she says. "I can hear sirens." She is crying. "Don't change your mind, Dex."

"It isn't," I say. "It is not too late."

I start moving. I am moving so fast I can hardly make out my own movements. I have never moved so fast. Nothing has ever mattered as much as this matters now.

"I haven't changed *my* mind," she says.

"It's different," I say.

My dad says, "It's too late. I probably deserve it, right?"

"No," I say. My hands are tearing out plants, and Tanis and I are moving impossibly fast around my dad, sitting on the pink bed, his new shoes flat on the floor.

I run outside to the back shed and grab the red gas can. *Danger*, it says on the side. *Highly flammable*. Tanis has the plants in the pit and my dad is still inside on the pink bed yelling, "Dex, for Christ's sake, come and get me. DEX!"

The gasoline glugs out of the can, splashing my shoes and my jeans.

I step back and Tanis jumps forward. She has a long match, like we used at the lake in the summer to light the hibachi. I back away. The flame is huge, it leaps up like a wave and for a second she vanishes behind it, and then I can see her again, wavering like an apparition.

Tanis is real. I did not make her up. My knee buckles. For a second I think I'm going to fall into the fire or be sucked into it.

I go into the basement and I pick my dad up and carry him outside. I put him a safe distance from the flame. Safe enough. And we watch it burn and time is running out and the smell is thick and heavy and we are going to suffocate, I think. But of course, we aren't.

This is not selectively edited.

This part is the truth.

It's possible that I can't tell the truth. I don't know what it is anymore. Or maybe I do know and I can't tell it because it is *too* real. Maybe I never did.

When you start to lie, it's easy to lose track of what is what. Sometimes it's impossible to know when you start. You think it's just that one wall, with the door and the tunnel and then suddenly it's a whole house, a whole city of tunnels and lies and none of it matters. You can't keep track because it's not trackable. The tunnels don't lead anywhere that you remember because you are busy remembering the lie.

That's how it is.

I think I started when I was five, riding my bike down the street, a book taped to the handlebars.

Fiction was the first lie that made more sense to me than real life.

Maybe that's when it started.

Something flaps loose in my chest and I cough and cough. I can't stop coughing. Tears stream down my cheeks. They aren't tears. I'm coughing.

They are tears. How much goddamn crying can I still have left to do?

"It's okay," Dad says. "Whatever happens, happens." The air is red and white and blue. Except it isn't. It's the lights. The sirens suddenly fill my ears too full and I want to clamp my hands over them, but I don't. The flames lick the blackberries and that's when I realize what I have to do. I don't know if I have time. I grab the gas can and start splashing the shrubs closest to me. I throw the match just as Lundstrom rounds the bend. I can tell he's smelling the air. The smell of the blackberries burning is so similar to the smell of pot that maybe...

Maybe.

My heart is pounding like crazy when the bush takes the flame and there's a *whoosh* so intense that I have to jump back. The blaze sighs and then recedes, and I look at my dad. He nods.

"What's going on here?" Lundstrom asks.

"Just doing some burning," Dad says, like he's shooting the shit about the weather, completely ignoring the fact that he's sitting half-slumped on the ground. The bottoms of his shoes are black, melted. "Damn blackberries. Only thing to do is burn 'em out."

"Blackberries," repeats Lundstrom.

"Anything else we can do for you?" Dad says, like this is normal. Seven cop cars. A fire twenty feet high. The smoke turns toward us and envelops us in a black hug. I can't breathe.

I can.

I am okay.

I am not okay.

"Guess not," says Lundstrom. "Unless you lose control of this thing. Hate for you to lose your house."

"We have control," says Dad.

"Yeah," says Lundstrom. "Speaking of your house, mind if I go in and look around?"

"You got a search warrant?" Dad says.

"Go ahead," I say quickly. I know what he'll see. The empty pots, the fresh dirt, the grow lights.

The tomatoes on the pink bed.

"I don't need to look," he says. "No search warrant, kid. Your dad's right."

"See you at the game," says Lundstrom. "Big game tonight, huh?"

"You bet," I say. "I'm not playing though. Knee injury." I roll up my pants and show him, and my knee is purple and livid.

"Shit," he says. "What the hell happened?"

And then Tanis is there and she looks like a kid, too young for this, for anything. She says, "Can I talk to you?"

Lundstrom is confused. "What?" he says.

And I can see Tanis getting braver. And maybe part of this is going to end the way it is supposed to end, after all. I can't hear what she's saying, but as she talks, I can see her getting lighter and lighter. And then she's floating above the ground.

No.

She's taking Lundstrom inside. Then he is coming out of the house with the box. The box. And she holds up her hand and waves a bit. And I really want for it not to be goodbye, but I say it anyway. I say, "Bye." And that's it. It's not a good movie ending, is it? There needs to be a UFO, hovering overhead. A hail of bullets. Someone, maybe me, dying slumped over the fire.

But me and Dad just sit there, watching the fire until the smell starts to make me feel sick, and then what we do is we drive into town and get some Chinese food. If this was a movie, that would be some kind of fucked-up ending, right?

Roll credits.

chapter 35
october 2, this year.

I get the camera from under the stairs. The battery is still alive and I don't know how that's possible, but it's true. Sometimes true things are harder to believe than lies. A good liar doesn't make things too complicated. He just takes simple ingredients and layers them together to make an interesting story. Take, for example, some corn.

Add a maze.

And an alien abduction.

A pretty girl.

Two pretty girls.

I take the camera outside and I press *Record*. It's as familiar to me as anything, but not quite, like when you're in the shower and washing your hair for the first time after a haircut and it doesn't feel like yours somehow.

I don't know what I'm recording. The smoldering remains of our fire. The corn, waving in the cool autumn wind. The clouds tracking across the sky like nothing happened and maybe nothing did.

Speed it up.

Slow it down.

Add a soundtrack.

A murder of crows.

Film inside the house. Inside the dollhouse. Go closer and closer. Zoom in until all you can see are the crumbs of what is left.

Dust.

Nothing is real.

The table is not real and the tiny yellow house is not real and my dad is not real and Tanis is not real and Olivia is not real and aliens are not real and I press the black mark on my arm and remind myself that I am not real either.

Poof.

Make it all a dream.

chapter 36
now.

You are clean when you decide to stop.

I am deciding to stop.

I am sitting in my psychiatrist's office, which is above a gas station just outside of town. He has boxes of Kleenex scattered around the room. Dozens of them. Like a patient should never be more than an arm's reach away from a box of Kleenex. I can smell gasoline. I never cry in his office. His name is Dr. Gleason. His office smells—apart from the gas—like nose spray and the dust that burns on old slide projectors, moth wings burning.

I show Dr. Gleason a film. It's a documentary. I'm going to call it *What Is Real*. It is about me and Tanis, Kate and T-dot. A drawing, perfectly to scale. A map with instructions. The way we held the boards and the corn fell in front of us like it was there the whole time, just waiting to become art.

It's going to be about how you have to be careful when you contrive an ending because nothing ever goes the way you think it will, unless it's fiction. I used to like fiction.

When I was a kid.

Dr. Gleason asks, "What now, Dex?"

I start to laugh. "I don't know," I say. I'm not lying.

I laugh more. The office fills up with those brown birds, hopping. I can't stop laughing. But sometimes laughing like that can make you cry.

Crying is a different kind of bird. Crying is crows calling. Crying is the blackness of water in the lake. Crying is in the needle.

No. Crying is in the bubbles, rising to the surface.

But you just have to follow them. And once you get there, you don't have to go back. You can start again.

And then.

chapter 37

CUT TO:

INT.—OFFICE OF MAIN STREET SCHOOL

Show Dex Pratt arriving late to school. He's not hurrying because he can't, his injury slows him down enough that rushing isn't an option. Show how he isn't hurrying. Zoom in on his knee. Use CGI to make it seem like the camera goes through the fabric. That way it's still real, it's just reality amped up.

Show Dex half hopping, half limping into the office. He's late, but he's always late. Show Dex picking up a bright pink piece of paper from a tray. Dex flicks the paper. Show how the sound fills up the empty room for a split second so he feels like he's not alone.

DEX

Stacey? You here?

Show how he's not alone. In a chair, in the corner behind him, there's a girl with a crooked smile. She clears her throat.

Karen Rivers is the author of fourteen novels, mostly for young adults. Her books have been nominated for a number of awards, including the Sheila A. Egoff Children's Literature Award and the Silver Birch Award. Karen lives, reads and writes in a yellow house near the beach in Victoria, British Columbia, and can almost always be found online at karenrivers.com.